Praise for Nathan Englander and

DINNER AT THE CENTER OF THE EARTH

"One of our more consistently brilliant, bold, and funny writers." —Dave Eggers

"*Dinner at the Center of the Earth* blends elements of spy thriller and love story, magical realism, and an all-too-real history of one of the world's most intractable problems: peace between Israel and its neighbors." —*The Boston Globe*

"It's difficult to describe Englander's novel without giving something away. There's a delicious puzzle that becomes evident as it unfolds. . . . As weighty and political as *Dinner at the Center of the Earth* seems, it's also a plot-driven page-turner." —*Houston Chronicle*

"We must now compare Englander to Graham Greene as well as Philip Roth. And he comes off well in the comparison." —*Jewish Journal*

"*Dinner at the Center of the Earth* illuminates the zealot's blindness, the patriot's struggle for clarity, and the enduring dream of a coming together." —*O, The Oprah Magazine*

"Englander writes the stories I am always hoping for."
—Geraldine Brooks

"Moving. . . . A twisty tale of spycraft and false allegiances unfolds, but what stands out is Mr. Englander's insistence on finding romance amid the violence and deception. . . . The ageless struggle between Jews and Arabs comes to resemble a desperate lover's embrace."
—*The Wall Street Journal*

"A literary spy thriller. . . . Englander is as wise and funny and original and moving as ever." —*Financial Times*

"An absolute joy to read. . . . A dark, profound meditation on the state of Israel and also a gripping thriller, full of twists and moral ambiguity." —*The Jewish Chronicle*

"A wistful fantasy of an impossible Israeli-Palestinian romance." —*San Francisco Chronicle*

"One of the very best we have." —Colum McCann

"A searing message about the difficulty of just action and human connection amid the ping-pong match of retaliation in the Middle East." —*Newsday*

"[A] complicated but masterful exploration of the many contradictions of the modern State of Israel." —*Haaretz*

"A riveting tale." —*The Austin Chronicle*

"Smart and intriguing." —*Library Journal*

"Striking. . . . A thought-provoking political thriller with some romance and cheeky humor thrown in for good measure." —*BuzzFeed*

"Clever, fragmented, pithy. . . . Englander is a wise observer with an empathetic heart." —*Publishers Weekly*

"Englander has produced a masterpiece of literary imagination that seems to mirror his own evolution."
—*The Jerusalem Post*

Nathan Englander

DINNER AT THE CENTER OF THE EARTH

Nathan Englander is the author of the novel *The Ministry of Special Cases* and the story collections *For the Relief of Unbearable Urges* and *What We Talk About When We Talk About Anne Frank*, a winner of the Frank O'Connor International Short Story Award and a finalist for the Pulitzer Prize. He is Distinguished Writer-in-Residence at New York University and lives in Brooklyn, New York, with his wife and daughter.

www.nathanenglander.com

Nathan Englander is available for select speaking engagements. To inquire about a possible appearance, please contact Penguin Random House Speakers Bureau at speakers@penguinrandomhouse.com or visit www.prhspeakers.com.

INTERNATIONAL

DINNER

AT THE

CENTER

OF THE

EARTH

Nathan
Englander

VINTAGE INTERNATIONAL
VINTAGE BOOKS
A Division of Penguin Random House LLC
New York

FIRST VINTAGE INTERNATIONAL EDITION,
SEPTEMBER 2018

The Library of Congress has cataloged the Knopf edition as follows:
Names: Englander, Nathan, author.
Title: Dinner at the center of the earth / Nathan Englander.
Description: First Edition. | New York : Alfred A. Knopf, 2017.
Identifiers: LCCN 2017011795 (print) | LCCN 2017016609 (ebook)
Subjects: LCSH: Political fiction. | Jewish fiction. |
BISAC: FICTION / Literary. | FICTION / Thrillers. |
FICTION / Jewish. | GSAFD: Suspense fiction.
Classification: LCC PS3555.N424 (ebook) |
LCC PS3555.N424 D56 2017 (print) | DDC 813/.54—dc23
LC record available at https://lccn.loc.gov/2017011795

Vintage International Trade Paperback ISBN: 978-0-525-43404-7
eBook ISBN: 978-1-5247-3274-5

Book design by Betty Lew

www.vintagebooks.com

Printed in the United States of America
10 9 8 7 6 5 4 3 2 1

For Nicole Aragi

There is accumulation. There is responsibility. And beyond these, there is unrest. There is great unrest.

—JULIAN BARNES

DINNER

AT THE

CENTER

OF THE

EARTH

2014, Gaza Border (Israeli side)

It's never about you. Neither attack, nor counterattack. Not the three boys kidnapped, surely dead, or the child murdered in the forest, burned alive.

Sitting still in a chair outside your rented cottage, you wait for the click of your tea water come to boil. You shift a foot, and, at sight of you, a lizard turns the color of the sand.

Across the country, the soldiers scrabble through the South Hebron Hills. They crawl about, hunting the bodies, turning stones. And here, beyond the fences, the Gazans strip the markets bare; dutifully, they run their taps, filling bucket and bowl.

It is light still, bright still. And you know, with the dark, the missiles will scream out from the olive groves and the rooftop blinds, from the hospital parking lots and the pickup-truck beds. The people along the coast will move into secure spaces in cities ever northward, mirroring the missiles' reach.

And you, you will stay in your chair, and sip your tea, and watch the arc of the fiery tails as they curl overhead. Then will come the sirens and the burst and spark of countermeasure when the batteries hit their mark. So close is your roost that your only worry is ineptitude, if the fighters on either side fire short. This rattle and boom is as of yet nothing but the sound of the two nations ramping up to the inevitable war.

This time, as with every time, when the fighting starts it will be more terrible than the fight that came before. Always it is the worst, the most violent, the least restrained, a steady escalation. The singular rule.

And once the invasion begins? There's no knowing how and when, or even if, the bloodshed will ever end. Only that both sides will battle for justice, killing each other in the name of those freshly killed, honoring the men who died avenging those who, before them, died avenging.

Because of all this, you understand that your own thoughts are unseemly. Your concerns outweighed and of no matter.

Is it your boy gone missing? Is it your son burned alive? No. No, it's not. And unless that's your soldier son sleeping alongside his tank at the border, your masked fighter, out-gunned and unprotected, manning the Qassams that whis-tle through the night, then we expect you will not wallow and will not mourn. You are to take your daily disappoint-ments, your unmet expectations and private catastrophes, and know that they are worthy of shame.

Of course, you *do* know this and have accepted it. At least, this is what you tell yourself, as a bird you cannot name swings low by your ear. It ends its glide and then pumps its wings.

In the silence that the bird breaks, you hear the sound of feather moving against feather during flight—a wonder. You turn your head to follow its path, shielding your eyes from the sun.

Sitting there by your tiny cottage, you squint and consider your own astonishing stupidity, your brutal obstinacy, your resistance to giving up your own unique and abiding want.

As the water gives off its audible roil and the kettle makes its click, you get up, telling yourself: You do not matter. Let it—let *him*—finally go.

But the imperative does not stick, and it seems that you will forge ahead with your truly hopeless undertaking. Until the right moment arises, until you get your lover's secret signal, you will, in the face of the endless, menacing unknowns, hold fast.

And to that inventory of silent surrender that this—that any—war demands, you've decided there is one loss for you, too large. A sacrifice you find yourself unwilling to make. It's a personal privation you can't stomach and will no longer accept. Let the soldiers soldier on and the civilians bear their burdens. But for you, you simply won't have it. You will not brook your broken heart.

2014, Black Site (Negev Desert)

Though they both know every millimeter of the cell in which they sit, every scratch in the cinder block, every factory-mixed fleck in the tile, the guard points back over his shoulder at the camera mounted above the door, encased in its casino-style tamperproof opaque dome, fixed there looking as innocuous as a big glass marble.

There is an identical camera on the opposite wall, above the head of the prisoner's single bed. That one is aimed through the Plexiglas door to the toilet and shower and also covers the thin metal shelf, with its books and bubblegum and English-language magazines (too wide for it), a cache representing the very height of the privileges the prisoner has acquired from the guard over the years.

A third camera is screwed in over the prisoner's sliver of an archer's window, watching—from a different vantage—the two other cameras that watch it in return. The window-wall faces the one the bed is pushed up against, the only one without its own source of surveillance. The guard always felt that maybe that wall was left blank because a fourth feed would constitute overkill to the overkill, as the window-wall camera alone, with its bird's-eye view shot through a fisheye lens, has every angle of that cell covered. With the other two units, every movement of the prisoner's life is recorded in triplicate—except for when he's in the bathroom, which, unseen by the camera over the door, its single blind spot, is recorded but twice.

Recorded and time-stamped and dated, marked with the camera number and the nickname for the cell, "The Peach Pit"—which the guard chose for no good reason other than he was home smoking a joint and reading the Hebrew subtitles of a *Beverly Hills 90210* rerun with the sound turned off when he got the call for the job.

Pointing up at that camera, the guard explains to the prisoner what it looks like to the guard when the cell is pitch dark, when the prisoner wishes he could feel that he was alone with his thoughts, when he wishes it could be for him pure, true night.

It is a shock for the prisoner, since, in the dozen years since they'd been hitched, the cameras, and the guard's view behind them, are the one thing, in all their searching, probing, absolutely endless conversations, that they never, ever discussed.

In response, the prisoner cocks his head and looks back at his guard most quizzically, for he knows his keeper would not be breaking his teeth over this for nothing. And the guard knows some things too. He knows that he himself is not as educated as his fancy fucking charge, and that his gift for metaphors is maybe not the strongest, though he's really been trying to use one as a way to soften things up, as a way to maybe take stock of their time together and then use it as a bridge to some very upsetting news—upsetting even to a disappeared, nameless American confined to a cell that doesn't, on any written record, exist.

That is, it is bad news with some bite.

In sharing the terrible news—a revelation for which the guard is in no way at fault—the guard will also be forced to share what he would call some *fashlot,* and what the prisoner would call "mitigating factors," that would color the story and reflect poorly on the guard, the prisoner's trusted— and only—friend. It might rightly jeopardize a relationship they've both treasured, in what they both understood to be a very Stockholm-syndrome kind of way, a relationship Prisoner Z liked to call "Patty Hearstish," a reference the guard had been compelled to look up.

In his own defense, as relates to the complication he hasn't yet copped to, the guard has only been trying to protect Prisoner Z this whole time. It was the very literal definition of his job; his title *was* the action itself. He's been guarding Prisoner Z in more ways than the prisoner could understand.

How, oh how, had it come to this! The guard recalls the first time he sat down in front of his three plastic-shelled deep-backed monitors—glowing; his own little triptych set up in front of him, with which to observe his secret ward. The screens were set up with one dead center, the other two touching and tilted in toward him a hair, each offering a different singular monochromatic perspective from which to watch the exact same nothingness going on in the cell. The way those monitors were angled, and feeling his own face lit in that blue-gray light, it reminded him of the way his mother used to hold a silver cardboard reflector under her chin to catch the sun by the sea, his mother, who would plop down in a beach chair and roll up her sleeves but still wore her modest skirt and her sandals buckled tight around her stockings.

It was she who had, way back in 2002, done him the favor of trapping him in this miserable bind. He'd screened her calls to his mobile and only answered the house phone— that is, her phone, the one his mother paid for—when she'd kept on yelling over the answering machine that she'd refused to abandon, though he'd begged her to switch to voice mail like everyone else.

It wasn't during a *90210* rerun that she'd rung him, but right in the middle of a show he couldn't bear to have interrupted. He was busy playing along at home with the British version of *The Weakest Link,* at which he was quite excellent, only ever stumped by the super-easy throwaway questions, distinctly British in nature, making him feel bitterly that—in the unfairness of geography and the misfortune of having been born into the armpit of the Levant—he was inevitably doomed to fail.

He felt this same dumb luck during his other favorite show, the British version of *Who Wants to Be a Millionaire?* Not a million shekels either, but a million British pounds—a windfall with which a person could really live a life. How was one supposed to study the things passively absorbed from being? Those simple offhand questions weren't about knowledge at all. They were freebies tossed in, gifts for those blessed to be born in a certain place at a certain time. And still, he made an effort to study up.

He had spent a lot of time in the army reading, trying to better himself and find a way to claw his way up in the broader world. His plan had been to get himself far away from Israel as soon as he could. You know what they used to say to each other back then? "Last one out, remember to turn off the lights." The guard had dreamed of ending up in London or Manchester, and, even if it was Birmingham, he'd make do. Then he'd get on one of those shows, where they'd tease him about his accent, and then he'd surprise them all by winning himself enough for a nice little nest egg to cushion his brand-new British life.

When his mother got him on the phone that morning, she wouldn't stop talking, even while the guard begged her to hold on, please, until they'd fucked up the chain of answers. He'd be happy to talk to her while they voted someone off.

"You'll end up in prison, one way or the other," is what his mother said, ignoring him. "I figure this at least puts you on the right side of the door. This way, at least you'll be able to come home on the weekends."

"It's Israel. We let the murderers come home on weekends. You could kill a dozen people and they'd let you out to dance at your kid's wedding. No sale."

"This is a special job," she said. "Top secret. You'll be a *shushuist*. You'll have a fancy résumé for the rest of your life. And the prime minister is asking. The General—it comes from him."

"The General is asking? For me?"

"For you alone. So you can imagine it must be a real emergency if he wants me to turn to you. It's something he can't go outside the circle for—and I really shouldn't even be talking about it on the phone."

"If anyone's tapping your phone, it's him or his fascists."

"Or the Russians," she said. "Or the Americans or French or your beloved Brits. Anyway, it doesn't matter even if they are listening. I haven't said anything wrong. Nothing at all."

"You're doing it again," he said. "You're talking for the transcripts. I hate when you fake talk for whatever country's spooks are eavesdropping."

"Okay," she said. "Sorry," she said. "I know I do that. I have a very strange job."

"You do."

"And now I have a strange job for my son. It will pay nice. And it can't be hard."

"How do you know?"

"Because the General thinks you're an idiot. He smiles when I tell stories about you, but I can tell, he thinks you're a fool. If it were complicated he wouldn't trust you. It's that you're loyal and can keep your mouth shut, is what he's after."

"Nobody keeps a secret better."

"Also, he doesn't think you'll ever find a girlfriend to whisper it to, even if you wanted."

"He said that, or you're saying?"

"Who is 'he'? 'He' we're already done with. Don't ever, after this, even think his name in relation to the work."

"Okay."

"Promise me not even to think it, yes?"

"I'm really hanging up now."

"Do! It doesn't matter. You wouldn't win."

"What?"

"If you were on the show, you'd lose. That's why people watch. On the couch, at home with a beer resting on their bellies, everyone knows all the answers. It's different under scrutiny. You don't have what it takes to handle the pressure."

"I do."

"Then prove it. It can't be long, this job. A couple of days, maybe a few weeks, at most—and he promises to keep you on the books for a year. No harder than babysitting a sleeping child. Soon as they figure out what to do with their problem, you can go back to watching TV. If you ever do wake up and want to build a future *in this country,* if you ever want to move out of your mother's apartment, a nice vague entry on the résumé, and the government payslips to go with it, it will make their minds run wild. You can go to high-tech after this. They'll think you were a top assassin, or a frogman. They'll think you're a hero even if all the General is asking is for you to keep a chair warm. And remember, it's *not* the General asking. Don't even think about him ever again once I hang up this phone—you already promised! Let me hear you say it!"

"I promise."

"What do you promise?"

"I don't even remember. That's how forgotten it is."

"Good," she said.

"Good," he said. "Tell them to call."

"I already did. Now go watch your show."

2002, Paris

He really shouldn't touch that newspaper, and really shouldn't be in this restaurant again, and definitely should have stayed on his side of the river, keeping to the relative safety of the Left Bank near his home.

In his sorry state, Z has come to the conclusion that he should never have passed any of the battery of psychological exams, that it was odd that he'd been recruited in the first place and ridiculous to have put him in the field. He still likes to believe that there's always wisdom shoring up the Institute and its secret systems, and imagines his handlers knew his weaknesses at the start but found there was an upside worth the risk.

Now they're facing the reality of their poor decision and will have to neutralize Z at great expense.

His garroting, or poisoning, or drowning in the Seine, would, in the annals of Israeli espionage, be the same as brushing a little Tipp-Ex onto a form. He is a human typo soon to be whited-out from his line.

He stops himself from following that train of thought any further. Open worry, panicked musings, they change the facial musculature, they make him seem guiltier and more suspect and might, in a weak moment, cause him to forget himself and look nervously around. Were there someone who had not yet spotted him, hunting for such a tell, it would be a giveaway of the most obvious kind.

He thinks it best to focus on respiration. He takes control of his breath, calming himself, inhaling and exhaling in a measured and natural way. He moves from the very-out-of-place Hebrew newspaper on the table over to the cash register, behind which—as per usual—a giant, scruffy man sits, looking like a French-Jewish Cossack.

What is not as per usual is the waitstaff. There is a new waitress—North African, he'd say; also Jewish, he'd say, who faces away from him as she bends over the tubs of hummus and tabouleh and labneh, scooping food onto a plate. There is also a tall and muscular new waiter, who is, on this visit, the person who concerns him most.

The moment that Z entered the restaurant, he noticed the waiter noticing him. The waiter immediately stepped out the side door, texting something curiously short into an already repocketed phone.

From the way the waiter holds himself, Z can tell that he hates his new job, and that he is maybe an actor or a musician, and that he also appears to be gay. Or maybe he is acting gay, and acting unhappy, and acting aesthetically bent so as to camouflage himself among the legion of like-minded Huguenot waiters who want to be singers, or painters, or directors of artsy French films, all of whom can't stand the tourists and touristy Jews they're forced to wait on all day in the Marais. It's *their* neighborhood now (gay, not Huguenot), and the sooner they close down this little living museum to the shtetl, or pack it up and move it out toward the airport and Euro Disney, the better.

It is the perfect cover, if this waiter-that's-not-a-waiter was expecting Z's stomach to betray him yet again. All he'd have to do now is step back outside and press some detonation code into that same phone. The next thing you knew there'd be Turkish salad on the ceiling, and Z spread all over the Rue des Rosiers, ground up into his own personal pâté.

Z can feel himself sweating and nearly hits the ceiling when the Cossack at the register asks him politely whether he wants takeout or to sit down.

Z tells him in his bad French that he wants to sit. The manager points to the open table by the window, the one with the paper resting atop. Z takes a seat and, considering the newspaper curiously, as if he's never seen a Hebrew daily before, picks it up and drops it onto the chair opposite, leaving it hidden from view.

Who brought it? Who carried it here, an edition two days old?

Then he remembers a story they all used to laugh about during his training. A story about one of the terrorist bigwigs whom Israel had tried and failed to assassinate— though not by much. The target had been successfully poisoned, but after weeks laid up in a Damascus hospital, he didn't succumb.

All the victim knew about his own near-killing, the only thing his doctors could tell him for sure, was that the toxin hadn't been ingested by mouth but introduced through his skin. He also knew that Israel was surely and actively still trying to see him dead.

What Israel knew was pretty much everything. Where he was at any given moment, whom he met with, and half the things he said. They knew it all, including the protective measures the man now took. Like some poor King Midas, afraid to make gold, this man had ceased to touch anything whose point of origin was unclear. When he got a letter, his most trusted aide stood in the other room and read it through the door. Food was carefully sourced, prepared on premises, and tasted in advance. Toiletries were replenished from a different pharmacy, in a different part of the city, each time. As with the food and the letters, this loyal aide would then run his boss's Right Guard up and down his own patriotic armpit and floss with the first minty meter of any new wheel. This same secretary also traveled to a new newsstand each and every day for a fresh copy of the paper. Then he'd turn the pages for him, as his fearless leader read.

Recalling this, Z uses his foot to push that chair and that poison paper farther away, feeling his throat go dry. He looks at his fingertips where they touched the newsprint. As the waitress approaches, Z holds them up to the window, looking for residue in the light.

What brings Z to this restaurant for the fifteenth time in the fifteen days since his plan's implosion (through explosion) and the betrayal of all he held dear is his weak stomach. It isn't weak in the traditional sense. For the sensitivity is in spirit, not digestion.

Under unbearable pressure, plotting an escape from his self-inflicted bind, Z found he desperately needed to eat the comfort foods that calm him and remind him, from the inside out, of his real and true self. When expecting one's own unexpected demise, isn't it fair to keep taking a favorite last meal, until it proves to be just that?

So Z further risks his already-imperiled life, unnecessarily exposing himself daily for a plate of hummus and a little chopped liver, for some smoky eggplant salad, a kibbeh, and a fat square of salty feta. He will—marrying together the two halves of his self—have a warm pita and a basket of rye bread, which is exactly what he orders from the waitress who is busy writing it all down in her pad. Taking her in, he acknowledges that—along with food—he has another kind of terrible weakness. It is that he also falls easily, and hopelessly, in love.

She is beautiful, dark skinned, and dark eyebrowed, and has above her perfect lips the tiniest black down of hair, the faintest of mustaches, that makes him think she is the most perfect woman he has ever seen. After he's done mangling the French language in his attempt to order, she shakes her head and addresses him in English. His heart melts again.

"My French is almost as bad as yours," she says, with a barely perceptible accent that leaves him melted into a puddle. "This will be better for us both."

And so he ventures it. "Italian?" he says.

"Roman," she says, wiping down his table with a rag and then lining up his silverware with a neurotic flair. When she reaches to straighten the other chair, she picks up and holds out the paper.

"Not mine," he says.

"Do you want it?"

"I'm staying away from the news these days. In any language."

"Well, my Hebrew is even worse than my French," she says, and puts the paper back where she found it.

"You're an Italian Jew?" Z is openly enamored.

"I am," she says. "And you're an American?"

"Sometimes, yes."

"And Jewish?"

"It depends who's asking."

⊰❀⊱

He crosses the river back to Rue Domat, his alley of a street and one of the quietest in the heart of Paris. A place easy to slip into and out of, a street with access to egress (by foot, taxi, bus, Metro, RER, even by boat), and so sleepy and odd a stretch as to make any aberration stand out. It was the perfect place for an operative maintaining a low profile, and living under a simple cover, to set up shop.

Before things turned sour, it had made Z feel safe when keeping an eye out for enemies from the other side. It served the same purpose now while on the lookout, with much greater angst, for those from his own.

Swiping his fob below the keypad, Z hears the click of the lock and slips through the gate to the building's archway. He nods at the woman sweeping in the courtyard and disappears into the entrance on the left, taking the stairs two at a time to his second-floor flat.

He makes all the checks of his training, and all the checks he's amassed from experience, and a mix of those one somehow absorbs and conflates from a lifetime of American movies and TV. Inside his apartment, he peers out the back window that looks from his bedroom onto the courtyard. He finds himself staring down at the top of the caretaker's headscarf as she sweeps her way toward the rear arch. He then runs to the front window to peer down both ends of the street. No cars, no bikes, nothing but the man who sits on his red suitcase, begging, at the point where the block elbows with Rue des Anglais.

Z has dropped two euros into the man's cup every morning he's been in town from the day he moved in and occasionally asks a question and hands the man a twenty-euro bill. He has been grooming him for the day he might need to know something good.

Satisfied nothing is amiss, Z strips down to his skivvies

and gets in bed to lie on his back and stare up at the ancient rough-hewn beams of his ceiling, looking for patterns where there are no patterns, losing himself in the gnarls that interrupt the grain.

It's his main form of entertainment since being viciously awoken to the consequences of what he'd done, for Israel, for Palestine, and, most urgently, for himself. He now sees his actions as a crime of political passion, undertaken in a desperate, last-ditch fugue state and driven by his good-hearted intent to do what's right.

The first thing he did in the aftermath was go around the flat unplugging telephone and TV and radio. The same went for the cable box and the outmoded Minitel that was already there when he'd moved in. He popped the battery from the alarm clock for no good reason, and, citing personal, murderous precedent, he removed the battery from his cell phone, along with the SIM.

He arrived at his office the next day, sweaty and uncontrollably nervous. He took a nightmarish meeting with his boss and handler and, sensing his paranoia was no longer paranoid, Z stashed his laptop in a drawer of his desk, its new permanent home.

With that, there was nothing in the house that could send or receive a signal, so staring at the ceiling is all he has. That, and a single French novel that he can't read, left on the nightstand when he'd rented the flat.

As he concentrates on the beams, trying to empty his mind, his thoughts veer to the severity of the situation in which he's entangled. By now, headquarters in Tel Aviv, and various bureaus around the world, have tallied a good part of the damage that he's done, combing through the files he's dumped, the operations he's blown.

All those angry *katsas* assigned to the French desk must

be falling all over themselves for the chance to torture Z, to find out what he's shared and whom he has betrayed, to hang him up by his toes, waiting for the secrets to fall out of his pockets like loose change, and then to wring out of him the reasoning behind his unhinged, treasonous exploits.

There's really no need to beat it out of him (at least from his perspective). Z would flip on his own. "I was trying to avoid a calamity on Israeli soil," he'd say. "It was the ticking bomb that justifies so much of the misery we unleash." Of course, this would not satisfy, as his bomb has blown. So he might also explain that he was trying to even the score. Unfortunately, the score he was trying to even out was the Palestinians'. He was trying to make amends for his sins. He knows that second part wouldn't go over. Recompense for one's enemies, well, that wasn't the point of spy craft at all.

Anyway, his abduction, transfer, and torture in Israel is the last of the options he thinks they'll choose. Z figures what they're really fighting over is the pleasure of being the one whom Z would see coming, of getting to witness the very real dread he would feel as he recognized the person sent to murder him with great brutality, or maybe just to render him useless—lobotomizing him with an ice pick or awl and leaving him to be discovered, a trickle of blood running from a nostril, his eyes differently lit, as he roamed vacant around Parc des Buttes Chaumont.

What scares him more than facing that moment of knowing are all the operatives skulking about that he wouldn't see at all. The cloaked killers. And, supporting them, the army of *sayanim,* the sympathetic-to-the-cause Parisians, who play their scaled-down roles. The locals ready to lend a spare room, or leave the keys to a car, the volunteers who, when tapped, are happy to act as another pair of eyes. Wherever he goes, every extra step in that city, he is exposing himself to these unidentifiable strangers who are surely already on the lookout for Z.

Failing to picture any viable solution, any permutation of a future that includes rescue or escape, he becomes so upset that he fetches a bottle of cheap supermarket champagne from the kitchen and, standing by the front window in his underwear and keeping watch on Rue Domat, he pours himself glass after glass, throwing them back until he's done.

Trying to take advantage of even a quick alcohol-fueled, nightmare-sodden sleep, Z crawls back in bed. He still can't stop the terror tapes from spinning and only calms himself by picturing that blessedly callipygous waitress bending over the hummus, scooping a heaping plate.

He had loved her, even before she turned around and approached his table. He had loved her coloring, and her eyes, and her big behind, and again that faint mustache that she didn't care to wax off.

Z flips over on the bed and buries his face in a pillow. He imagines an impossible new life, the pair of them forgetting everything that came before, and together looking only toward a bright new after. He'd recover all the money he'd stashed away for just such an emergency, maybe moving with the waitress to some flat up a hundred flights of stairs. Z can see her in their living room, the skylight open, the rain blowing in. Eyes closed, straining his mind, Z can see it, and Z can hear it. There is the waitress, her belly pregnant, her little chest turned huge. Then comes the sound of their fat, smelly pug, asleep on the couch at her side, and snarfling through its flattened nose.

2014, Hospital (near Tel Aviv)

Let us first listen to the sounds of the fat man endlessly dying. The beep and whirr, the hiss, pump, hiss of it. An adjustment is made, a suctioning and clearing, and then we are back to the endless electrical rhythm of the machines.

Ruthi smooths at his blanket, tucking a corner, when the night nurse arrives.

"I don't like it," Ruthi says. "I don't like the way he looks."

The way he looks? The night nurse raises an eyebrow, stepping back to consider him—this big bear of a man in his big mechanical hospital bed. She cannot see a lick of difference from the way he looked last night, or the night before that, or in the weeks or months or years that preceded.

She tries her best to appear deferential to Ruthi, who is neither doctor nor nurse, not even a relative, but some sort of functionary who'd become indispensable to the man during the height of his powers and, at low ebb, is still the one whispering into his now stroke-deaf ears.

Both women are private hires of the General's sons, who insisted—even in this fine institution—that their father live, at every moment, with someone by his side.

The nurse, under Ruthi's gaze, closes her eyes for a moment and considers the cadence of the General's steady machine-fed breathing. Then, touching his cheek with the back of her hand, she takes his temperature in the way only one who truly knows could. No change to him. This she lets Ruthi know with a glance.

"Well?" Ruthi says, waiting for some kind of diagnosis.

What can the nurse say for the nine thousandth time, when nothing at all is amiss, when the great general lies there on his bed, waxed and rouged like a Red Delicious, looking like a fat Lenin on display. Their dear departed murderous leader, whose family will not let him die.

What can she say to appease this unrelenting worrier, who—the nurse is convinced—has kept the General alive, year after year, solely through the power of her constant declarations that he was about to be dead?

"Has the doctor been by?" the nurse asks, hoping only to engage and calm Ruthi and then usher her from the room.

"Of course the doctor has been by," Ruthi says. "It was Brodie today, and what does that old fool ever see? He runs an intensive care like he's getting kickbacks from the morgue."

"Didn't he say anything?"

"You think I listen when that walking death sentence talks?"

Ruthi glowers and takes up a towel, which she uses to wipe at the edges of the General's mouth. She checks all his tubes and feeds, the ins and outs of them; she drums with a fingernail at all the digital vitals flashing on their tiny screens, as if to increase their accuracy with a tap.

The night nurse, God help her, would have pulled the plug on this whole operation long ago. She is sure there are plenty of folks waiting for the General down below. Scores to be settled in the afterlife, long-dead enemies sharpening swords.

Still not satisfied, Ruthi leans over the bed's railing and presses her lips to the General's forehead. "I'm telling you, he feels hot to me."

"Maybe it's you that's a little cold. The room tonight—"

"The room is fine. It's him that's not right. Anyway, it's not your concern, because you know I'm not leaving."

"My shift—"

"You can forget your shift. Head home."

"Now, Ruthi," the nurse says. "Any longer and you'll miss your bus to Jerusalem. You can sleep with your phone under the pillow. I'll text you if an eyelid so much as flutters. Eight years in that bed. Without a word. Without moving."

"The eyes, though, when they're open . . . and the first finger, when his son talks, or when I read—"

"Yes, yes. He's ready for the Tel Aviv Marathon. I'll sign him up."

Ruthi scowls, full of affront. "Something changes and no one sees. The doctors are blind to it, you are blind to it."

It's clear on the nurse's face that she marks no difference. "You look tired, is what I see."

"I'm not tired," Ruthi says, now trying for tenderness. "Honestly. You go. Sleep an extra night for once. Anyway, tomorrow is my day off—easy for me to see the week through."

Ruthi takes a step forward and gives a friendly pat to the back of the nurse's hand. In that touch, it is the nurse—who indeed notices everything—who thinks, yes, it is Ruthi running cold.

Ruthi, like the rest of Israel, had watched him from afar for nearly the whole of her life. In his last years among us, when he was actively ruling, and leading, still stomping about and warring, she had—more than most anyone—the privilege of serving at his side before that became the literal embodiment of her days.

Sitting by his bed, she never saw any quantifiable change to his warm, gray, seemingly empty self. But Ruthi could always tell when his soul was leaning back her way. There was no way to explain it. She could sense when his mind stirred and swam up, peering out from just below that shimmering surface. The body that held it quietly chugging away.

When the worrying sons asked, or the doctors, when the occasional reporter who still remembered tried to get her to shed some light, she would not use the image of water, or talk of his soul as if it were a kind of man lost in the woods. She would tell them that he suddenly fills up the room and then is gone just as quick. A consciousness rolling in, like a storm coming through.

When this did not suffice, which was always, she would simply revert to the stories she'd been raised on. She would recount the tale of King Saul's visit to the Witch of Ein Dor, of Elijah appearing at the cave of Shimon bar Yochai. Her point was that spirits far more removed than his have long, in this land, returned to advise. That before Heaven and before Hell, before those newfangled Christian notions became all the rage, there was another place where souls rested after life was done. The good and bad penned up together without judgment, and always within reach for counsel. If that was possible, how much more likely was it that the General was somewhere alert and at the ready, especially when his body—a wonder—still hung on in our world?

"It is a time of grave danger for the nation," Ruthi would say, when her telling inevitably turned to a plea, "and the Jews left rudderless at the helm." Sounding desperate, she'd say, "Everyone's moved on, and him, right here, ready to lead."

The listeners would nod kindly, or nod politely, or nod with an understandable indifference. Often, that nod might hold a contempt that Ruthi was unafraid to address.

"The *answers* are in there," she'd say. "*In* him. There has to be an expert somewhere who knows how to ask and get answered."

She could see how they regarded her, a sad soul herself. They treated her as a ghost in the room.

It was a lesson in how power shifts. When the General was seated behind his desk in the prime minister's office, his laughter bellowing out through closed doors, the waiting heads of state would curry Ruthi's favor, wooing and deferring, knowing that, more than the General's generals, or his cabinet stooges, the woman who worried over his snacks and his ChapStick, who made sure his hotels had the right pillows and that his plane never, ever took off without the newest pictures of his grandchildren stowed aboard, that she was the one who could best get Israel's obstinate, unyielding leader to hear the other side.

On the days when the medical staff listened to Ruthi politely, she would point them to the Bible she read daily by the General's bed. This should be their only guide, she'd tell them.

They would prattle back at her in the language she'd become fluent in. They would talk of in vivo connectivity and corticothalamic function, reference the newest research and the unpublished studies that they always spoke of as being on the horizon, as if ideas rose up from behind the ocean every morning along with the sun.

Scientifically, what they held to be absolute and undisputable when it came to the inner life of the General was, even more than Ruthi's religiosity, still a matter of faith.

That night, with Ruthi beside him, is not a peaceful one for the General. There is only the crack of the gun, the one shot, one son. A fever dream is what we'd call it, if we could still call it dreaming. A simple, horrible nightmare, if he were asleep.

But he is neither of those. He is living in the infinite, ever-present unendingness of that single shot. Of all his bullets fired, of all his endless wars, all of existence for the General is a bright sunny morning, reading the paper in the den, and then that crack rippling the calm. The one shot he did not fire is the one that now keeps firing, a ball set loose from a prize Ottoman gun.

"Lily!" he calls. But she does not come.

He had heard a shot. He had been hearing that shot, lifting his head from the paper, turning an eye toward the sound, while judging distance and caliber, playing the echoes off the hills and fields of his farm.

He is already calculating return fire, judging how a bullet aimed might bend and drop on the currents of air, his body lit by every susurration of October breeze.

He's already mapped where his own weapons are, knows how much ammunition he has, and counted off those whose lives he might be responsible for in his midst. All of this takes place outside of language, and outside of thought, assembled in another kind of consciousness. And all this information is processed and acted upon within an instant, even less—a gift that, when coupled with a great amount of luck (or some kind of mythic national fate to which he was inextricably tied), has kept him alive, has gotten him through what he should not have survived, leaving him in the fall of 1967 in his den, with a newspaper, and a hot mint tea—already cooling.

And a bowl of salted almonds.

And a bowl of fat figs.

It is those bowls in front of him, the sight of those bowls beneath the edge of his newspaper, the stain of salted fingers smearing newsprint, that tells his mind where he is, tells him that he has heard a shot but does not need to dive for cover, does not need to scramble for his gun, does not need to defend or conquer, and so he begins to lift his head and calls, "Lily." But Lily does not come.

It is the lifting of the head that seems to go on for centuries. This is the part that he cannot make sense of.

That shot—it never seems to go away.

2002, Berlin

It is ridiculous, Farid knows, to compare this perfect, placid lake to the ocean, or these tiny sailboats of mahogany and teak to the floating bucket he'd learned to fish on as a boy. But, still, sitting out on the dock in the evening, watching the sunset drawn out across the water, it reminds him of home—an idealized, dreamy version of his miserable, embattled home.

He sits on that dock, behind a mansion on Lake Wannsee. He is a member of a small yacht club, made up of the aforementioned fleet of classic, pristine boats.

One of the perks the membership affords him is a prized right-of-way. He has a key to a modest gate nearly invisible in its plainness, set as it is among the puddled iron entrances to the manses of Am Sandwerder. Through it, he may walk along the narrow path between two towering residences and, climbing down the hill, reach the little marina where, of late, he sits more often than he sails. He comes now a few evenings a week.

He'd heard of the place through a friend of a friend, who

knew that he'd grown up "sailing." Farid had laughed out loud at the word.

What he'd grown up doing, he'd said, was surviving.

He'd been born into a formerly landlocked and land-loving Ramla family, refugees who'd been driven to Gaza by the Naqba. First his grandfather and then his father had eked out a living working other people's fishing boats, learning the craft, before they'd squirreled away enough to buy a broken-down boat of their own.

It was on that boat that Farid and his brother had learned to haul the nets, mend the nets, how to pilot the boat and fix an engine, which, more often than not, meant knowing where to hit it with a wrench to start it up again when it conked out.

He also learned where to find fish when the Israeli Navy declared a blockade or a high alert, when they moved the accepted mile marker back to where the trawling was harder and where you could—with the Palestinian fishermen anchored side by side—practically skip from the deck of one boat to another all the way back to the beach.

It was from that family boat, nearly a decade prior, that Farid had been willingly plucked up and hauled over the bow onto another, larger ship while out at sea. While the Egyptian smugglers reached out their hands, it was his brother who steadied the boat, who made sure Farid did not fall into the sea. It was his brother who'd said to him, "The big fight is yet to come. We will need money, we will need strategy. We will need distant bases, manned by those who look good in a suit." Farid had laughed at his brother, who smiled back, sad. "You could never take a punch," his brother said. "I will do the warring, and you can fight the fight from afar." Then the Egyptian smugglers who'd taken him on, and taken the money he'd saved for years toward that purpose, gunned their engines and aimed the bow toward Spain, from where—no thanks to those pariahs—he'd eventually made his way here, to Berlin.

Farid didn't have two pennies to rub together back when he'd been mistaken for a yachtsman. The night it had been said, his stomach was grumbling from hunger, and his back hurt from the grunt work he'd been doing, but he was wearing the suit he'd just bought—for he understood that his brother was right. He had a look to him that would work in his favor, if ever he got the clothes to match.

"Not sailing, but surviving," he'd said in response, and his friend's friend had laughed and given him a happy shove. From then on, Farid dreamed of the day he could call himself a sailor, and he was driven toward that day by the dreaming itself.

He knew then he would find a way to make enough money, beyond what he needed to live, and beyond what he needed to send home, and beyond the great sums he'd need to provide for the cause, if he'd wanted to guiltlessly join his friend's friend—as there was an invitation involved—at the "little yacht club, not even yachts, really. A rinky-dink operation, a few boats barely bigger than Sunfish." This oasis (which was anything but "rinky-dink") was out on the edge of the city, along the necklace of lakes that curled up to the forest, with the airport and the autobahn—the empty stands from the AVUS's racetrack days—just on the other side of the trees.

Farid made a name for himself in business, importing and exporting his way into the upper economy if not the upper class. He moved what needed moving to make money. And moved what he might to help his fellow Gazans in their plight. And so that his money might make money on its own, he'd invested in the markets and exchanges of the world. He bought stocks. He bought real estate. He owned part of a bowling alley in Manhattan, and a grocery store in Blantyre, which took in almost as much on a Saturday as the government of Malawi itself.

Farid finally wore those fine suits and got himself expensive haircuts that other rich people might note. And, despite a drink now and then, and a woman, when a woman would have him, he still went around with the welt of the faithful man marking the center of his forehead and, aside from his brotherly commitments, paid his own personal *zakat* many times over each year.

When he'd felt secure in Germany and German, as well as with his wealth, he pushed his way through that gate and walked down to the lake and the boathouse. With great confidence, he'd told the Japanese man who ran the place that he'd grown up on the water.

Dressed, once again, for the part he wished to have, he lied about his proficiency, twisting his wrist to show off the weight of his fancy watch, as if this might hypnotize Takumi, who actually didn't seem to care at all, amiable man that he was.

All Takumi said was, "Take me out for a sail."

The pair set out in a quick twenty-six-foot Soling, the lone vessel that belonged to the club itself. Farid failed miserably at his certification run. As he did, Takumi just smiled and cheered him on, and helped him raise the spinnaker and helped him not get killed by the swing of the boom, and did not allow him to drown them both, when it seemed, with barely any wind to push them, that he still might upend them. It was the perfect mix of Japanese politeness and fault-finding German unspokenness, so different from the frank, no-nonsense ways of Farid's rough-and-tumble youth.

It made Farid love this man, who allowed him, in a dignified manner, to come clean and admit everything he had said was false. That's when Takumi said, "Even better! I love to teach."

It was as vulnerable a moment as Farid had had since leaving home.

Other than the fact that Takumi, without irony, referred to himself as "The Commodore" when addressing yacht club–related matters, Farid found him to be an excellent teacher and an easygoing and generous man.

After that, the two of them went out twice a week, sometimes three. Takumi told Farid he was a quick study. Farid had never been happier than at that time, fully engaged in the moment, and at complete peace, cutting through the water with this magical fellow, in this magical place, with one man speaking in Japanese-accented German, teaching another with his Arabic-accented German, how to sail from what was the American International Yacht Club based on a lake in Berlin.

Four years later, Farid felt as comfortable, and knowledgeable, as anyone else who belonged.

Comfortable enough to come while away the evening as if it were his own stretch of waterfront, as if the mansion up the hill behind him were his own. And as he once had pictured himself occupying the spot where he now sat, he now pictured a day where a house like the one looming high at his back might also be his.

But mostly, when he was out there sitting, Farid simply was. It was the only time he managed to shut off. He'd always thought meditation must be like prayer without God. But, sitting on the edge of that lake of an evening, he'd come to understand it was something like this.

On quiet nights, when there was a little wind coming up, barely enough for him to read the ripple on the water, he'd watch the boats rock in their moorings and listen to the perfect sound of those halyards hitting against the masts, and ringing out like bells.

Since the start of the last Intifada, in the long months since the Israelis began leveling Gaza and the West Bank, Farid would come to the water near daily just to breathe and to try not to feel guilty for the wonderful, peaceful life he'd built. He thought of his brother fighting the fight, and all the young warriors by his side on the front lines, and of all the good and peaceful people whose lives were upended. Farid had always taken comfort in the part he played from afar. And he'd turn red, and turn hot, at his hubris and greed, at all he had ventured, the free money of the tech boom wiped away in an instant. And now, when he was needed most, he had nothing to give.

On nights like this, when thoughts of the uprising—and the attempt to crush that uprising—would not leave him by the lake, when thoughts of his own extraordinary missteps would not abate, he'd make a game out of his hopes, like a little boy. A fact by which he was embarrassed and a little bit ashamed.

He'd pretend the path from the street down to the water, running between the two grand houses, was a right-of-way between the dry hills of the West Bank and the beaches of Gaza. That's what peace would be like if there ever were two states.

If he was feeling momentarily heartened, he'd dream of a complete Palestinian victory, of the Zionists driven out and back to wherever it was they came from. What heights would Jerusalem reach, he would think, if it were ever united under a green Hamas flag? He need look no farther than his adopted city, than beautiful Berlin. There was no end to what a city could achieve without East or West, but thriving as a singular, vibrant whole.

2014, Limbo

The General is startled by the shot and looks back over his shoulder, at the patterned wall hanging behind him. Something Lily has hung. Many-colored, woven of yarn, some sort of local craft, like an unfinished coat. Whether Indian or Mexican, he does not know.

It is not the weaving he has twisted his head around to see. It's not to peer out the window at the burn barrel smoking at the edge of the fields and clouding the view beyond.

Perplexed, for he cannot recall why he has turned, he finds himself staring at the hardy ficus in the corner of the room. Healthy, healthy, with its green, thumb-fat leaves. His Lily could make anything grow.

He is frozen staring at that plant, struggling to recall something, his head still turned, the tendons of his neck stretched taut. What he remembers right then is the Latin. A ficus is the same family as the fig tree.

And the General finds himself looking back into his lap. Beneath the paper, balanced—a bowl of salted almonds.

A bowl of fat figs.

There is a gun missing. That's what he's been looking for, why he again cranes his neck. It's the sound of the shot that has reminded him. That old embossed prize of an antique gun, and the wrought-iron brackets that hold it affixed to the wall, empty, above Lily's weaving.

Where has it gone, his treasure?

The gun was given to him right after the war, a Janissary's rifle, a trophy retrieved from the Syrian front.

Such craftsmanship he'd never seen before in a weapon, the vernacular tradition at its murderous best. This one had an octagonal barrel, the stock sheltered in ivory, and a five-sided brass butt end, inlaid with polished stones. All that fanciness, and still simple. The barrel bands looked, at first glance, to be of gold thread, but—and he thought it a lovely bit of restraint on a weapon so ornate—upon inspection, they were made of some sort of sturdy twine.

As soon as he'd been given it, he'd walked his visitor out to the gate of his ranch, and, without going back into the house, the General climbed into an Egyptian jeep that he'd driven back from the Suez, another keepsake. With the rifle as his passenger, the General raced over to the blacksmith who did all the ranch's ironwork and shoed all the horses in his stable.

"What can I do you for, General? Something broke off that jeep?" They are old friends, the General and the black-smith. The blacksmith is also an orthopedist in Be'er Sheva when not living his country life. He and his neighbors all wear multiple hats, their identities defined by the uniform of the day.

The General runs around the front of the jeep with his

heavy, thumping plod. He reaches into the passenger side and brings the rifle to the blacksmith, who wipes his hand on the pair of fatigues he wears under his leather apron. "Magnificent," he says.

"I want to hang it," the General says. "In the living room or the den. Something pretty for the wall."

"You could have just called to tell me you wanted to put up an old rifle," the blacksmith says. "No need to lug it."

The General, not one you'd ever call sheepish, turns his eyes down and says, "I wanted you to see."

For the blacksmith, it's a simple request. He already has two perfect brackets ready. But he wants his friend to be happy—a hero, a legend now for the ages. And a modern blacksmith owes spectacle to his patrons. Everyone wants to see the searing metal hit the bucket and hear the hiss of steam. He pumps his bellows and starts the show.

If this wasn't the dream of Israel incarnate, the General thinks, watching. Here is this man, hammer to the anvil, the socialist dream, the hot sparks flying, the iron embers sitting red, sticking like mosquitoes to the leather of his bib. In perfect complement, two French-built Mirages come screaming overhead, the jets' wingtips marked with the Jewish star.

They are heading south to the Suez, the Sinai ours up to the edge of the canal. Suddenly there is a country big enough to justify a flight to get from one place to another. A country whose perimeter can't be patrolled on foot between breakfast and lunch. Now they are a nation with defensible borders, not too skinny at the neck, with that head always begging to be lopped off.

Here these Jewish pilots, Israeli pilots, flying those Mirages down across the desert—some of the most advanced technology in the world. And the General down on earth, caught up in this ancient practice, smithing in an ancient Jewish land—revived.

There were new words for everything in their dead language put back to use. New words for the jets and their radar systems. New words for the tanks and the radios inside. But for this, for the hammer and beat of the forge, the Bible still sufficed.

2002, Berlin

Farid is alone at the marina but for an old man, puttering around in the cockpit of his boat, tinkering and polishing and drinking a bottle of wine. He offers Farid a glass, which Farid declines, though the gesture takes him away from thoughts of war and returns him to a peaceful state of mind.

He sits in his preferred spot, at the far edge of the dock, beneath one of the linden trees that overhang it. He has settled in to admire the lake, his back against the retaining wall.

No matter how long Farid lives in Berlin, he's still amazed by how late the sun sets in summer. Twilight seems to stretch on forever, as the blue of the water deepens and the orange haze lining the sky above the forests on the far shore glows.

It's not long after the other man leaves that Farid—relishing his solitude—gets up to go. As he brushes off the back of his trousers and takes one last look at the lake, he sees the club's Soling, tacking jaggedly toward the marina's last open slip.

He knows who it is, for he has been watching this terrible sailor for a week. It pains Farid every time, though he can't help but watch, sometimes from between the fingers of his own hand.

Farid stays as the captain poorly trims the sails and poorly steers his craft. As the boat closes in, Farid isn't sure if the ineptitude hasn't now turned into a controlled assault. The man seems to regain the most minimal control, which is then promptly lost. If not for the bumpers he remembers to toss over the sides, and a final adjustment as he steers his way in, Farid expected to watch him go down with his ship.

When the man moors the boat, he tangles his lines and ties them sloppily.

Fully pained, Farid finds himself approaching.

He says, in German, "Can I help?"

When the man doesn't answer, Farid tries English, at which the hapless sailor brightens up.

"I know I'm a mess," the man says.

Farid does not disagree. He only nods and unties the bow line, before slowly, didactically, leading him through the motions.

"First, you always start under the . . . horn?"

"Cleat," the man offers, happily. "In this case, with boats, that's a cleat."

"Then, always, first, it's under the cleat."

When the man nods, Farid makes his figure eights, ending with a slow, obvious underhand loop.

"You always want to finish like this. Then you pull the free end tight-tight and coil it so it looks neat. No loose ends," he says, to show that he knows some good phrases, and that his English is more than up to par. "Not in Germany, and not with boats. Everything, always, nice and tight and clean."

Farid is about to make a joke about American ease and American indifference when the man moves toward the next cleat to refasten the line as he'd been shown. It's then Farid sees the insignia woven into the man's jacket.

"You're a Canadian!"

"How'd you figure that?" the man says, surprised. "Everyone here calls me American, even after I tell them where I'm from."

"The Bluenose," Farid says. "On your jacket. Pretty much every Canadian who passes through here to sail is wearing a Bluenose jacket or shirt, or wears a Bluenose hat on his head."

"We're a proud people," the man says, as he tries and fails to cleat the stern line properly. Clearly thinking better of another attempt, he hands the rope to Farid. "But not too proud to recognize when we're outclassed."

Though the Canadian did not exactly grow up poor in Gaza, neither did he grow up rich, as did nearly everyone else who ends up trodding that dock. He'd been a regular kid, the son of a dentist, who'd flitted around the lake in a friend's fiberglass fourteen-foot dinghy, while growing up in Montreal. He'd crewed in some races over a couple of summers half a lifetime ago. Now, doing a stint in Germany for work, and with no friends, and no language, and some time to spare, he is suddenly back to the boats.

He says he's renting a house on the lake, which can only mean that he—or his enterprise—is very wealthy. He says he saw the yacht club through his telescope, and thought, with time on his hands and sweet memories of sailing, he'd give it a try.

All this he shares between observing Farid retying the stern line and coiling the tail. They walk the path together, up between the mansions, and out onto Am Sandwerder.

"So, which house is yours?"

The man points back out across an expanse of water that they can no longer see. "If you walk down the street until you get to the Saudi Arabian embassy," he says, "I think mine is, more or less, directly opposite."

The man then clicks a key, and a car beeps somewhere down in that direction.

Farid says his good nights and turns to go. He starts walking for the train station and doesn't make it two steps before thinking of Takumi, and all the kindnesses shown to him when he was new in town.

It is also, he knows, the right thing to do. He thinks back to his schooldays and recalls the story of Abu Talha and Umm Sulaim feeding what little they had to their guest in darkness, so that they might pretend they too ate by his side.

The Canadian is already walking off, and Farid calls to him awkwardly, speaking at a clip.

"I'm not sure if you want to travel into the city now when you're already so close to your bed," Farid says, "but I was going to get something to eat. If you want to join."

In an instant, the man is at his side.

"If you thought you were going to get away with being polite and then disappearing, you messed up good." The man claps Farid on the back, as if they're already familiar. "I've been surviving on doner kebabs from outside the train station, and any fruit I can eat without peeling. A decent meal would be an absolute joy."

"There's no kitchen at your house?"

"There's a kitchen about the size of a football stadium. But it holds a mean little troll of a chef who is offended by my palate and who's convinced I shave off my taste buds every morning after brushing my teeth. It's classic German, all cream and meat and gastronomic foams. If I ate that stuff every night, I'd either have a heart attack or explode. I miss my neighborhood in Toronto. I miss having a good quiet place on the corner where I can eat a green salad and have a drink."

"So what are you hungry for?"

"Honestly?"

"Of course."

"Anything ethnic—but not German ethnic. Mexican. Italian. Thai."

"How about Chinese food?"

"I would pretty much die for some Chinese."

"Good Friends," Farid says—which he understands, by the man's expression, sounds more like a proclamation than the name of a restaurant. "It's in Charlottenburg, right down from the Paris Bar."

When his guest shows no sign of recognition, Farid says, "You really are new here."

"I am. And I'm in your hands," the Canadian says. Then, looking a touch embarrassed, "I'm a good businessman, I promise. But I'd make a terrible politician. I already know you too well not to know your name."

"Farid," Farid says.

The Canadian's name is Joshua—"Call me Josh." When Farid asks if he wants to join him on the train, the Canadian holds up his keys and says, "You're going to shit when you see the car they got me."

They order a whole sea bass baked in salt, cold noodles, and spicy tofu. The Canadian orders shumai, and har gow, drinking ice-cold pilsners along with it, one after the other. Farid figures he must already be too drunk to handle the astonishing sports car in which they arrived, though, in Joshua's speech and his manner, it does not seem to show.

They talk easily about their families, and their child-hoods, and a lot about sailing.

Takumi had not offered the Canadian any lessons after taking him out. "I was good enough to eke by," he says, "but not bad enough, apparently, to have lessons forced on me. I was lucky. The wind was right where it should be whenever I went looking."

"It's hard to be lucky with sailing," Farid says, refilling his tea. "I'm surprised he lets you take the boat out."

"Considering what you saw?"

"Yes, considering what I saw."

Joshua smiles and laughs and toasts his host, knocking his beer glass against Farid's teacup.

"I promise, I was bad that day too. But it was the ideal, shining version of my badness."

Farid likes this man. There is something charming about him.

"If you want," Farid says, "I could give you a lesson or two."

"I couldn't," Joshua says.

"It would be my pleasure," Farid says. And he finds, as he says it, that he really means it. "It's a slow time for me. A distraction would be a favor."

Joshua raises an eyebrow, holding Farid's gaze, and giving him what feels like the chance to back out.

"Choose a morning," Farid says.

"This week I'm traveling on business. But next week, I'm around."

"Fantastic," Farid says. And, not wanting to pry, for he's not one who likes to be interrogated, he still asks Joshua what he does that brings him all the way here.

"Trust me, it's boring. It'll ruin a perfectly good meal."

"You know what my father used to tell me? The more

boring the business, the more money there is to be made. He would walk me by the biggest houses in Gaza and say, 'There is the man who makes cement.' 'There is the family that puts the buttons on your shirt.' We'd stand outside this huge villa, and he'd say, 'That whole mansion is built from hummus and pita, one customer at a time.' I was so little when he'd take me, I actually thought that house was made of hummus, spackled from floor to ceiling."

"I hear you," Joshua says. "Honestly, it's just dull. I'm basically a junk dealer."

"A junk dealer, with a hundred-thousand-euro car."

"More like a hundred fifty. That sports car has the added sports package built in."

"From selling junk."

"From importing and exporting that junk, I guess. Resale is maybe the best way to put it. Anyway, the car is leased."

"Still, it must be a big lease," Farid says. "And import and export is a big umbrella. A lot of us fit underneath it."

"I sell used computers. Used cell phones. Used copiers. Anything with a chip inside. Which is why I should try and sleep a few minutes. I need to wake up when Beijing does and start working the phone."

"You're not on Canada time?"

"This horrible octopus of a deal—the part that's killing me right now is with the Chinese."

Joshua reaches for the bill, and Farid stops him, insisting.

His guest is clearly touched and says, "It won't make up for it, but why not come for breakfast before we sail. We'll let that evil chef clog all our arteries, and then you can teach me to tie a proper knot."

2014, Jerusalem

Ruthi's son sits in a chair at the edge of the balcony, his feet up and hanging over the rail. He's out in his boxers and a pair of flip-flops, and Ruthi can smell the woodsy, bubble-gum odor that's mixed in with the tobacco, her son smoking a joint on a Friday morning and taking in the day.

The guard doesn't put it out at the sound of his mother's approach, only cracks open his eyes, one at a time, as if it's better to absorb her in stages.

"You didn't come home last night," he says.

"And you didn't call to see why."

"I already know why, don't I? Same as always—you were worried your boyfriend might give up the ghost."

His mother raises a cautioning finger.

"*Halas.* Don't be disrespectful."

"Now I owe him respect? Do you know how many nights I almost got killed because of his crackpot politics?"

"During your service?"

"Yes, during my service."

"What danger did you face? You demolished terrorists' houses in the night. Houses don't fight back."

"You don't think that's a crazy job? Sneaking into some village with a bag of explosives and leveling homes?"

"If the terrorists were still in them, maybe. But this is the relatives. These are the houses where the already-dead terrorists once lived."

"Which raises its own issues, no, Mother? Giving five-minute warnings to old women who never race out the door with anything but their olive oil and a picture of Arafat? It's pitiful."

"How else do you punish someone who's already gone? It's a deterrent."

"Do you think so?"

"I don't have to think so. I'm not the one who did it, you are. Do *you* think so?"

"I was doing my service. That was my job."

"So it's a deterrent, then."

"No, it isn't. I think it's an incentive. I think it's a fucking terrorist recruitment campaign."

"So now it's your fault when they send us terrorists?"

She loves to do this, his mother, to dispense her clipped and nagging motivational speeches and unasked-for life advice. Much like the blowing up houses, her son thinks, his mother's talks seem to have the opposite of the intended effect.

As to this age-old argument about the usefulness of the General's many crusades, they were both careful to stick with the latest uprising, so as not to slide back to Lebanon and Tyre and the war from which the father he couldn't remember hadn't returned.

The guard closes his eyes and takes a pull. He needs a moment to self-medicate before engaging again.

He counts down in his head, and then blows a long puff of smoke toward the Knesset across the way. He blinks away the dryness before turning to his mother, who now leans back against the railing, the panorama behind her.

"I think it's the General's fault," he says. "That whole shitty Second Intifada and the ruined future that's followed. And let's not forget the prospect of all the spectacular shittiness yet to unfold."

"You blame both the past and the future on the General? That's quite a lot of power to afford someone. Maybe you respect him more than I know."

"When you torpedo peace, it reaches both ways."

"The lost peace you put on him too? On the General who pulled every last one of his beloved settlers out of Gaza, as he once did in Yamit? The very father of those settlements and the only one to take concrete steps toward withdrawal? That is your enemy of progress?"

"When telling the Palestinians different mattered most, he took a thousand men up to Haram al-Sharif to let them know who's boss. The Second Intifada was just them telling him back something different."

"Again with the thousand men and that stupid walk up the hill?"

"It's symbolic. Symbols matter. They give shape to a time," the guard says. "Shape to the abstractions."

"Shapes to abstractions? From your mouth?" His mother is not having it. "You should only be so smart. This," she says, waving at his words as if they still hang above him along with the smoke. "It's because you sit all day babysitting that brain in a cage. What you just said, it comes from him. I can tell."

The guard gets up, frustrated, and grabs hold of the rail.

"Better to babysit a brain than to babysit a body."

His mother takes hold of the balustrade beside him.

"No, son," she says. "Not a body. I babysit a dead man so

powerful, he continues to live. You, you sit over the living, already dead. A coward who earned his spot in the dark."

"I'll agree that he's an idiot, but he's actually sort of brave. He risked everything, and lost everything, for what he believes."

"What *does* he believe?"

The guard looks to his mother, embarrassed. "He never says."

Ruthi pats her son sweetly, lovingly, on his pale, pale arm.

"It bothers me that you truly don't understand the world and yet somehow think you do. What worries your mother is another generation of Israeli men like yourself, who think they know it all and don't have a clue."

Ruthi moves away from him, shifting over to the plastic window boxes hanging from the railings.

One of the planters is completely overgrown with giant flowering basil. Ruthi snaps off the tops and starts to pull the dead leaves. She talks without turning.

"You're beyond ignorant, my left-wing son, if you think the Palestinians needed the General to start that Intifada."

The guard laughs out loud at this. "Left-wing? Mother, I'm a secret prison guard, and a Golani soldier, and a Beitar fan. I listen to the Shadow on my iPhone and vote Likud every time."

"Your point?"

"I'm only saying, the right has moved so far over that, from where you stand, I look left."

Ruthi snorts at that. "Well, don't call the Temple Mount 'Haram al-Sharif' in my house. It already has a name, a Jewish name." Ruthi lets the handful of yellowed leaves she is holding drop from the balcony into the empty, garbage-strewn lot below. "And know that the last Intifada was inevitable. If you don't believe me, ask any Arab. They were looking for an opening and the General gave it to them. They could have stayed quiet. They could have kept their casino and their airport. They could have had a capital right here in Abu Dis. They could have had near everything they wanted. And they threw it all away."

"Sometimes, almost what you want just isn't enough."

"Fair enough. Only remember, it was your mother who had to welcome the parents of our murdered schoolchildren. Your mother who had to sit with the parents of the soldiers whose bodies were dragged through the streets. Their protests left a lot of bodies, and a lot of survivors that your mother had to lead into the General's office, so he could tell them their children hadn't died in vain."

"Now your boyfriend is also a social worker?" And now the guard can't control himself, now he goes where he shouldn't. "Let's not make the man behind Qibya, and Sabra and Shatila—"

"In Beirut, he only turned a blind eye," his mother says, stopping him. "It was the Phalangists who did the killing."

"A murderer, Mother. A butcher."

"I know what he did in the past," she says, "same as you. But that same General saved this country from certain destruction many times."

"No one disputes that."

"But your mother is trying to tell you something else. I'm trying to tell you what the General had planned for the future. He'd have given you and your Palestinian friends just what you wanted. He'd have saved this country for good too. I know what would've come next. If only—" she says.

"If only he'd lived?"

"If he'd gone on as he was. The General was going to make two states. He was going to make peace. A tactical choice as strategic and painful as war. Peace was the bomb the General was going to drop."

"You really believe that?"

"If he ever finds his way back, he'll end up looking more lefty than you."

The guard shrugs and takes a pull off the joint, extinguished. He lights it and pulls again, holding smoke, and then offers it to his mother, an invitation she's refused a thousand times. "Try it," he says. "I promise, it'll help you calm down."

She demurs, but it makes Ruthi think. "You know what?" she says. "Go fetch your mother a glass of wine."

"For breakfast?"

"Look who's talking. I've been up for more than a day. I think, in this instance, it's all right."

The guard nods. He goes off toward the door, and Ruthi watches his beautiful, skinny self, her son in his worn briefs, with his amateurish tattoos horribly prominent wherever she looks—dolphins and tigers, a child's choices etched onto a grown man.

The guard returns with an open bottle of white wine from the fridge and, along with it, a box of chocolate wafers and an empty jelly jar for a glass.

He finds his mother already sitting in his chair and goes back and drags out another to join her. She drinks in silence, and he smokes in silence, and they eat the cookies together.

It feels quite lovely between them, and at some point they both tip their chairs back and both hang their feet over the edge of the balcony's rail. They stare out over the city, a span of red-tiled roofs and then that beautiful carpet of cypress and evergreen trees stretching out toward the Jerusalem Hills.

2014, Limbo

A dozen. Ten dozen. A hundred dozen Egyptian tanks rolling in. Four times that number in armored vehicles, and another four times that in men. A Yom Kippur bloodbath, as thousands of Egyptian troops bound across the Suez. Their engineers drop bridges and the infantry swarm. They clog the canal with rubber dinghies, bear-crawling up the berms on the Israeli side. If God had split the sea for them, they'd still not have gotten across that fast.

And what do they find waiting at the Bar Lev Line?

A few score Israelis dug into holes.

The General stares into the sandstorm churned up by all that movement. Like a curtain draped across the world, tawnying the October sky. Last time he was down here— right here—it was as peaceful as an empty beach. Nothing but silence, so that he picked up on the drumming of its little feet as a yellow scorpion scuttled across his boot. Now the ground shakes from the noise as if from an earthquake that never ends. And with all that billowing sand as backdrop, making the light so strange.

Ruthi reads to him from the Bible, the portion of the week. She cobbles together her own version of the *Hayom Yoms*, psalm and song, prayer and piety, and whatever commentary of the ancients she can uncover that is relevant to the goings-on of the broader world. Because of this practice, she has become learned and sage.

Growing up in Darb al-Barabira, her oral tradition was drawn from the kitchen. Her lessons learned from her mother as Ruthi sat in a corner, grinding away with mortar and pestle locked between her knees. Her family had stayed after so many others had gone. And she knows she has it in her, a hereditary ability, in the face of all hopelessness, to hang on and believe.

The General knows they could've turned this war around at the onset if they'd taken the position at Missouri during the first three days. He'd arrived there to find a quarter of the Egyptian heavy armor blasting away. Infantrymen swarming, a force that quickly grew beyond counting.

He has not slept from the start of the fighting, hunting a route to rescue that still eludes. How the Egyptians were able to breach. How they sneaked up without sneaking— with the government watching every move. It is the thought he is mulling when his scouts bring back word. Water cannons, do you believe it? Embankments a hundred feet high, and the Egyptians use water to blast their way through. They laid their pontoon bridges at eventide and drove through the fresh valleys they'd made.

A moon in early evening and then pitch-black until dawn,

perfect cover for a crossing. And the Jews anyway distracted by penance, their stomachs stuffed for the fast, and their heads chock-full of atonement.

He had warned Military Command about the Bar Lev forts months before. "Sitting ducks," he'd told them. "Mobile defense is the only way." They ignored him. His ideas too big, his plans without respect for scale or budget or boundary. His record filled with rashness and ruthlessness and missions too costly for both attacker and attacked. "Look at the Vietnamese," he'd said. "Look how they strike, light and quick and unencumbered. If we can catch Egypt off guard," he'd said, not knowing that surprise is exactly what the Egyptians had planned.

The General pressed on and on, brawling in the war rooms as he did in the wars. He would not stop until Command paid him heed. They gave in. They were making changes. But, like everything in Israel—a two-year wait to get a telephone line—here, along the borders, the forts were half shuttered and the mobile units still locked in place, beached and unprepared.

All his warnings, and always they told him, "Don't worry, my friend, the Egyptians are weak. The Egyptians are frightened. Look at how they bungled '67."

Ruthi reads to him from Jeremiah, and she reads to him from Isaiah, stressing the appropriate passages again and again. "Who else but you 'with the breath of his lips shall slay the wicked'?"

She takes the sponge on its stick, a little lollipop of pale yellow foam, and dips it into a cup of glycerine-thickened water. One sip going down the wrong tube could be, for their fearsome, unstoppable leader, his end. She reaches over and wets his cracking mouth, splitting and scabbed at the corners.

"Come back," she says, openly begging. "Come finish what you started."

Southern Command had set up flamethrowers along the canal, a child's imagining of a solution. They were going to send the Egyptians running from jets of fire, toast the enemy up like bread. And where is this man-made inferno? The General focuses his binoculars in the distance, though he knows the answer. No gas. No flame for the flamethrowers, while the Egyptians, with their water cannons, come rolling through.

The enemy, they fight beautifully. Batteries of SAM-3s to keep our air force at bay. The Saggers tearing everything to shreds. All of this, it must be the Russians, and the Germans, and maybe some brand-new Libyan planes in the sky. A shopping spree is behind a war like this. The Egyptians push ahead like real soldiers—they have been training hard over the last six years. No motivation like humiliating defeat. They must hear every splash of a Jewish dive into that Red Sea water, every sizzle of a kosher steak on the grill, every moan of Jewish romance on Israeli cotton sheets amplified, all of it on seized Egyptian land.

The General comes to an immediate decision. It's time they forge their own passage back into Egypt. The Jews made it both ways before, they can find their way again.

He will find his own lane between enemy battalions. He will sneak along it and surprise the invaders, attacking from behind. It was a brilliant Egyptian assault with a brilliant

Egyptian defense, but somewhere there must be a gap in the rampart.

The General can already see that, while the Egyptians fight well, they are already drunk with success. They probably only planned to take the eastern bank of the Suez—and no more. But they already taste progress, taste victory. Sadat must have his eyes set on liberating the Holy City, on Jericho, on every name mentioned in the holy books.

The General is calling for maps. Demanding aerial photos. He is sure the Egyptians won't see it coming. They won't envision a tap on the shoulder and then a punch in the mouth. He will find a way to cross, and then, like Moses, he will hide in the reeds.

The General can picture it already. The first of Sadat's soldiers to remember his sweetheart, to pull a photograph from his breast pocket, the first one to shed a tear thinking of flag and country, all full of national pride, he is the one who will be first to turn back toward his beloved Cairo. And what will he see? Who will he find there but the Israelis charging his way.

Ruthi knows the Messiah will come at a time when all Jews are good. Or when all are guilty. And to the General she says, I don't know if we'll ever get closer to one of those days than right now, yes? Either the world is right or we are right. Greater Israel, either our greatest pride or our shame.

Ruthi dips her sponge.

Ruthi wets his lips.

Maybe that's what you wait around to see? A born competitor. You need to know how it ends.

The General stands where he should not stand, out in the open in front of his troops. His radio operator says, "Before the medic has to put you back together, sir, would you mind, maybe—" And this is when the tank right next to them takes a hit.

A Sagger missile sneaks right into that wedge of negative space under the scoop of the turret. A weak point on the Pattons, a fatal little fissure between the moving parts. It's what he hates about the M48. Its top section sitting there like a melon rind, with that vulnerable edge curving up. The tank rears back, throwing its front end off the ground.

The General watches the blast waves rippling, the way one watches the heat billowing off a tarmac, the pulses of energy barreling toward him. He feels himself lifted from the ground. His radio operator is tossed up into the air along with him. The boy, upended, looks like a turtle with that unit strapped to his back. Side by side, they seem to be airborne a very long time. What they both notice—for the General points downward and the radioman nods—is that the space where the radio operator was begging him to move is now under a tread of the tank, and that tread swallowed up in a ball of fire. In recognition of this, understanding, the radioman turns to him in the air and shrugs.

He is aware that it is taking too long to land, and the General laughs at himself. Such a heavy man, what a mighty explosion it must have been to throw him this high. Always on duty, the General cannot resist taking advantage of vantage. To be able to peer down at the war, to see the battlefield laid out. It's an opportunity not to be lost.

The General turns again to the radio operator, still sailing through the air by his side. He can see that this brave boy is frightened. Not battle frightened but scared of this strange flying. The terror is clear on his face.

A leader must know how to lead in every situation, and the General, taking charge, reaches out. He takes hold of the boy's hand and he says, "Look at me. Just look at me." The General says, "Tell me, from which part of the country do you hail?" When the boy answers, the General, who knows every inch of the Promised Land, all of it his home, asks a follow-up question, sweetly specific to that place. The boy locks eyes and, still agitated, begins to calm. The General, who never suffers remorse over a battle, finds himself, in mid-flight, feeling a rare pang of guilt.

He feels bad about enjoying this restful soaring while the boy clearly endures. "I have an idea," the General says, hoping to make things better. "Maybe it would be nice to hear a song?"

"I do not sing," says the radioman, "unless, of course, that's an order."

"No, no," the General says, shifting the weight of an arm, and then a shoulder, to turn himself toward the boy. He does this in the way one might when rolling onto one's elbow to talk to a lover in bed.

From this position, up there in the air, the General pantomimes fiddling with knobs. "The radio," he says. "See if you can get a station."

"Sir," says the boy, "it's not that kind of transceiver."

"Come, come," says the General. "That sounds like defeat. That sounds like the attitude of a soldier fighting to lose. Why not give it a shot? How can you know, until you try?" The boy hesitates, and the General continues to egg him on. "Flip a switch," he says. "What about that button you're always paddling at on the side."

The boy pulls the body of the radio around front, careful not to drop it. He turns the knobs and, with a bit of fine-tuning, he holds up the handset right there between them. Out of it comes music, Arabic music. It is Umm Kulthum, the legendary singer, so legendary that both of these flying Israelis are already familiar with the ballad they hear. A song so famous even the Jews cannot not know it. "We are very far south," the boy says, apologizing for the station. "No, no," says the General, tilting his head, bringing his ear closer to the receiver. "It is a lovely song. Let's listen." And together, they take in this plaintive voice crooning in Arabic, and they fly.

2002, Paris

He shouldn't have gone back to the restaurant to find her. Not the first time or any of the days that followed. He'd kept returning, though the waitress had never appeared again. Neither had that horrible, threatening Huguenot waiter, whose vanishing Z had taken as a positive sign.

He told himself that the visits weren't about her. He was crossing the river simply to satisfy his cravings for eggplant salad and poppy seed cake. He was exposing himself on those walks because, except for those lunches, he was left hiding in his apartment on an as-yet-uncommenced emergency family leave, a long-dormant excuse that was supposed to be Z's fallback means of escape. His boss had invited him to kick it off early, which Z accepted over showing up at the office to act bizarrely normal, while being treated with threatening normalcy in return. He was afraid to drink a cup of tea there, or enter the bathroom or the stairwell, or to be out of view of the many coworkers who had no idea what his cohort at their company really did.

Hunting for a better out, Z would run through every alternate scheme he could come up with, from mad dashes to the American embassy, to plastic surgery, to faking his own death. But he knew how his pursuers worked, because he worked for them. It was chaos theory and game theory and psyops and all the best intelligence and counterintelligence whisked up together. He'd think a plot through and then reverse engineer his own behavior in light of theirs, and then, working his way back forward, he'd map the steps he'd need to take to extricate himself from this bind in the face of their counter to his counter to their counter. He could see nothing better than his original plan, already muddled, which would have already seen him flown home to tend to his sick and dying mother, who was absolutely fine.

He was losing his mind, he knew. He was rapidly going stir-crazy, harassed by the cycling of his own nightmarish thoughts. The best way he could describe it, the image that arose for a man who spent his time studying his room, was to think back to the walls of his first hovel in Jerusalem, the one he'd shared with his roommate, Yoel, while they were both studying at Hebrew U. When the rainy season started, the apartment walls would first turn very cold, and then very damp, and eventually, battered and battered by the rain and the wind, they would bead up with moisture, never drying, as wet inside as out. It would get so bad, you could run your finger along them and scoop up the water.

At each spot where a droplet formed, a little black flower of mold would eventually bloom, and, as the winter dragged on, they'd open out, spreading and connecting up, until, by the middle of the season, the whole of those walls had turned black.

That was what was happening in his mind, Z knew. With every day of worry and every day of waiting for what-he-did-not-know-and-could-not-fathom, he could see the quality of his thoughts changing, the bad ideas beading up and starting to glisten. He could feel the temperature of his consciousness shift and sensed the first black spots on the surface of his sanity taking hold.

He tries to steer that Jerusalem memory to one of happier times, to warmer days up the mountain at the university, to sitting with Yoel and drinking beers in the empty amphitheater at the back of campus, the two of them silent, marveling at the sandy hills dropping down to the Dead Sea, and staring out over the heights of Moab and right into Jordan. Those peaceful thoughts, even when he reaches them, won't take hold. Those perfect moments in that perfect place are all, for him, now ruined.

Disconsolate, he trolls further and further back, trying to map every decision from childhood onward that had put him in this mess. How could he have ended up here? How had a little, religious, Jewish-American boy from Long Island become an Israeli operative, living undercover in Paris, and now a traitor to his adopted state? How could he have ended up being so many kinds of people at once?

Z, with a hand over his mouth, pulls at his face, despairing, surprised that he suddenly has an answer. At least, as to how and when it all started. He has found the seed. The instant he'd discovered that inside one, there could as easily be two.

He is maybe eight, maybe nine, walking home from Ace's candy store in West Hempstead, his sleepy suburb, with a Hershey's bar in his pocket. And he sees on the street where the anti-Semites live, he sees the big boys out in force, the tough kids, and the mean kids, wearing their denim jackets with patches, and their denim jackets with the sleeves ripped off. And him, in his saddle shoes, and him in his kha-kis, the line visible on his pant legs where his mother has let down the hems.

It is then that Z discovers in himself a propensity for the life he has ended up living. For he can remember the little-boy judgments he made. He is already too close to turn around without catching their attention, though they do not consciously acknowledge him yet. Confidence, he decides, is his best bet. He will walk a straight line, maybe nod his head when he passes, the safest route. There is only one problem. He recognizes, as if outside of himself, that his whole identity, the only one he's ever known, is that of a tantalizingly beat-up-able religious Jewish child, with a yar-mulke pinned to the very head he's about to nod.

That, right then, is the first time he does it. With a prac-ticed motion, as if he's done it a million times before, his arm swings up, and the hand—the hand with which Z now cov-ers his own mouth—slides up across his head, as if smooth-ing out his hair. In one perfect action, the yarmulke is gone, palmed, and slipped into the pocket, where it's swapped out for the chocolate. Suddenly, like that, Z is as Gentile as them. He feels it, because he has become it. And they, who would beat him on another day, pay him no mind. For Z is someone else, another child, passing with the candy bar that he's already unwrapping.

Even this memory, in its sweetness, is too much, con-sidering all its attendant personal pain. Z cannot anymore handle his loneliness, or his isolation, cannot bear the tenor of his thoughts.

It is evening, and morning is infinitely far off, and his lunchtime outing somewhere further. He cannot go on this way, and though he's previously weighed the risks and found the plus side wanting, he will head out after dusk. He

isn't going far, and he isn't going for long, and the peril outside his apartment seems better than what he faces inside
his mind.

If only Z had known in his perfectly lovely rooms in
Paris what he'd come to know in his single cell hidden, he
guessed, somewhere in the desert. If he'd had an inkling in
that breezy French apartment of what true boredom felt like
and true loneliness, and true limbo—what it might actually
be like to be locked up, hidden away without hope. If he'd
tasted real madness at that point, he'd not have decided that
he was so bored and so crazy that, without TV or radio or
a suitably advanced French, at the very least, he deserved a
taste of the night air and something decent to read.

With the summer sun forever setting, Z dresses in the half-
darkness. He pulls on his jeans and peers out both windows,
and heads down into his alley of a street.

Z rounds the far corner and walks speedily downhill,
past the little movie theater, to the churchyard park. Crossing through, he stops for a moment beneath what is known
to be the oldest tree in all of Paris. Some things, he thinks,
have survival in them. Some things stand, against all logic
and all likelihood.

He stops a second time at the fountain outside the bookstore. He cups his hands beneath the trickle of water. He
drinks, and splashes his face, feeling happy to be out in the
world.

The crowds across the way still teem in front of Notre-
Dame, and the tourists stream through the front door of the
shop. Z relaxes just a hair. It would be an impossible place
to take a life in any of the standard and messier manners, a
difficult place to drag him into a van.

Z circles the ground-floor labyrinth, making a pile under his arm, then climbs upstairs to see what else he might find. It's here, straight down the narrow hall, that he sees a woman standing on her tiptoes and reaching for some high-shelved volume, her back and beautiful behind turned his way.

He knows immediately who it is, and he knows that he is in love for real.

Of course, he shouldn't approach. He should take it as an ominous sign. After all, wangled coincidence, contrived serendipity, this is his bread and butter. It is how they do business, in his business.

But, really, how could this woman end up on the second floor of the bookstore, her back to him, and already up on tippy-toes reaching? That would be too good, and too polished, and the fact that he is even considering the machinations of it is only a testament to the rotted-through-with-paranoia workings of his brain. Also, a mitigating factor: seeing the waitress again was all he'd been wishing for and dreaming of, maybe even more often than he fantasized about strolling down a bouncing gangway and stepping across the threshold to a direct, JFK-bound, New York City flight.

When the waitress lowers herself onto the flats of her feet without a book in hand, Z is already over, tapping her on the shoulder.

"Long arms," he says as she turns. "I have them, if you need."

"Only browsing," she says, and, taking in the sizable stack he holds, "I'm not as decisive as you."

"I read fast," he says, and, considering the pile himself, standing there awkwardly, "I'm kind of a homebody these days."

The waitress, plainly feeling his awkwardness, stares down at her shoes.

Raising her eyes, she points toward one of his novels. A big fat copy of *Lonesome Dove*.

"That's exactly the sort of book I've been meaning to read."

"This?" he says. "You want to read about cowboys and cattle for eight hundred pages? In English?"

"I do. I've been thinking about America a lot."

"You have?" he says, too excitedly, as if it meant she were thinking of him. Trying to erase that question, to back away from his eagerness, he says, "Can I buy it for you, then? I'd like to."

"You can. But that would be odd." Then, attempting greater clarity, the waitress says, "I think maybe 'forward' is what I mean. Or 'intimate.' It is a strange offer from you. 'Odd,' yes? Does that make sense?"

He imagines she is going on because he has not properly responded. It's not that he's misunderstood. It's that Z is doing his best to listen, trying to maintain eye contact, to engage with this woman. The waitress seems to have chipped a front tooth since he last saw her. And Z just wants to stare at that chipped tooth for a lifetime, preferably without interruption of any kind.

He apologizes for making so forward an offer and then offers to buy it for her, still.

The waitress lets him. And the novel goes into a tote along with all of his. From there, they walk the neighborhood, and she accepts when he invites her for a drink.

They sit at Café St. Victor, one of the infinitely repeated, nondescript but effortlessly special bistros in the city. They joke and laugh and trade stories. They drink Kir Royales and eat fries, both talking nonstop, their conversation quieting only when he gazes at her lovingly or when she, having decided on dessert, is besotted by her chocolate mousse.

He asks her about her particularly excellent English, which was extra-particularly strong for an Italian. "Yes, we're unparalleled in all of Europe for not caring how good our English is," she says. "There's a small, private bilingual school in Rome, and that's where I went."

"Is someone American?"

"My parents thought it would give me an advantage."

"And has it?"

"It's made this date especially nice."

They have such a lovely time, such a warm and open time, that it surprises neither of them when she follows him home. He brings her back to his apartment, not caring if she knows where he lives. In fact, he desperately wants her to know where she might find him. Terrified that if she slips off, he might lose her again.

They sit on his sad sofa and kiss for a long time, and talk for a long time, and then kiss some more. They move to the bed, and take off some clothes, with the waitress firmly returning Z's hands to him whenever they stray too far. Z, overcome with excitement, kisses her and kisses her, happily losing his mind in a completely fresh and different way. They doze, with Z drifting off overjoyed. At some point in the night, they drowsily kiss some more, before falling into a deeper round of sleep.

When Z opens his eyes in the morning, he cannot believe that the waitress lies by his side. The light shines brightly through the arched bedroom door, and a softer light brightens the room from the courtyard-facing window.

The waitress opens her eyes, feeling his stare, and pulls the pillow over her head.

"That was fun," she says from underneath. "All that kissing."

"I thought so too."

She lifts a corner of the pillow to look at him. "Then we're in agreement," she says, lowering that corner and going back to sleep for quite a spell.

Z runs out to the bakery for a baguette de campagne. He stops at the open-air market for fresh yogurt in little glass jars that make him feel even more in love. He buys fruit from three different farm stalls, berries and peaches, and a watermelon, which sends him into the closest shop for Bulgarian cheese.

He sets out the whole spread on the apartment's old wooden table and then hovers between the arch of the bedroom door and the kitchen, so he can start on a coffee as soon as she stirs.

When the waitress finally stumbles out, she's wearing her underwear and his T-shirt, the one he met her in last night.

In place of a "good morning" Z says, "After I saw you at the restaurant the first time, I hoped, every day, that you'd come back."

"They stopped giving me shifts. The day I met you was my first and last."

"Sounds like waitressing may not be your greatest strength."

"It does, doesn't it," she says, sitting at the table and popping a berry into her mouth. "But maybe it's yours? Let's see how well you wait on me."

Z scoops and steeps and plunges. He pours the coffee into a bowl and brings it to her at the table, with a towel folded over his arm.

"How am I doing so far?" he says.

"Excellent service. I'd come back to this place."

"Would you?" he says. "Honestly?"

She looks at him, taking real time to consider.

"I've never dated a Jewish boy before," she says. "We have kind of a shortage in Rome. But the way you act so vulnerable and so needy, the way you're so polite and unaggressive in bed, all of it together is really sexy to me."

"So you'd see me again?"

The waitress bites into her bread and takes a sip of the coffee, and she tells him to get her some butter. When he presents it to her on a saucer, she looks into his eyes, and— the whole of it, as far as he's concerned, whistling through the space of that broken tooth—she says, "Who knows? I just might."

2014, Limbo

Never has the General dispatched a single soldier for glory or sport. His detractors accuse him of spending their brave sons on nothing—when it is he, more than anyone, who values each and every life.

The problem is that his most careful sacrifices still look like recklessness if one ignores a central fact: The General is tasked with fighting their wars.

And wars are fed on men.

They'd used him as scapegoat from the beginning. His own prime minister acting aghast, Ben-Gurion pretending he couldn't grasp what the General had always, in every battle, made clear. He was fighting to win.

The General would kill ninety and lose nine. He'd recede from a field of battle strewn with dozens of dead, carrying the two who were his back home. No other unit in the world fought with the General's numbers.

Whipping boy or no, the General's job has always been to deliver vengeance. They'd hint coyly and speak in hushed tones when they needed something done. And when the

General returned? They'd shake their heads and bury their faces in their hands while he stood before them, victorious.

Never did anyone give a direct order. They simply let him loose as if he fought his own private wars.

After every routing and reprisal they'd tell him, You cannot keep winning so well.

"Winning so well?" the General says, and looks to Ben-Gurion, who gives no response. He turns to Dayan, who offers him the eye patch, tilting his seeing side away.

Peres sits silently in a corner; ever the diplomat, he lets the other two men speak on his behalf.

Ben-Gurion says, "They kill one of ours and you run off like Samson to bring back a hundred heads. The world will not take it. The enemy's losses are too great."

"Then let them stop killing the one. Let them stay on their sides of the borders and I will stay home and sit on my hands."

Ben-Gurion talks to the General as an uncle might. He has always kept the General under his wing. "Do you understand what you start? You shame them in front of their people, and in the eyes of the world. They shoot a farmer off his plow, and then it's you running riot, invading. Then come the reports with my breakfast. 'He's burned down a police station.' 'He's slaughtered a whole unit on patrol.' It's too much!" The old man pulls with hopelessness at his crazy tufts of hair. "You cannot level a village with the people still inside."

Dayan finally speaks, to warn him. "Continue on, and the region will spin out of control."

"Perfect," the General says. "Spread the word. Tell the

Arabs, if they lose control so will your general. Tell them, I can't be contained. No one, surely, wants that."

Peres clears his throat. He says what the General imagines he must already have been contemplating. "It's not only our enemies. It could come from an ally. From the Americans or the British. There is a lot at stake, and any of them may find a way to put you out of commission for good."

The General laughs at this, a deep, satisfied laugh.

"Tell them I can't be killed. Not ever. Tell them all, 'He is more golem than man. The General cannot be stopped when he is out avenging Jews.'"

Peres, in his fancy French suit, twists uncomfortably in his chair.

The General leans his elbows on the table and points at Dayan.

"You, more than anyone, know it's true. You've witnessed too much to say different. How many times on the battlefield has that one good eye of yours seen me not die? You tell them," he says. When Dayan doesn't, the General says it himself. "I sit here, still breathing, only because Death cannot get a good hold."

The General straightens up in his seat, letting the challenge stand. He waits for an answer, sitting there in his white civilian shirt, open too far at the chest, his sleeves rolled up on his powerful arms.

They can see for themselves the scars and lesions and burns. They know from that first war alone, the cicatrix beneath his clothes cut wider and worse.

It was more than a miracle that he survived Latrun.

They consider him, because the General makes them. And they understand that maybe what the General says is true.

2002, Berlin

The spread Joshua is renting is more impressive than Farid imagined. He'd have been proud to live in the gatehouse, let alone in the giant edifice that sat across a statuary-strewn football pitch of a lawn. Weathered green bronzes have been placed all along the way to the front door, and through that massive door is a marble entryway with sculptures of its own.

It's a shockingly fancy abode. But Farid absorbs almost none of it as Joshua leads him right on through to a giant sunroom that juts out the back of the house, sticking deep into the yard like a thumb.

The room is all white, and what isn't white is window looking out onto the water. There are white couches and a white ottoman. There's a white table and chairs, carved with curling leaves and vines.

A telescope mounted on a tripod stands by the wall of windows, and Joshua motions for Farid to look through it, which he does, focusing on the yacht club on the far shore.

Farid straightens up, and the two men stare out the windows with nothing but lake unfurled before them.

"Sit," Joshua says, insisting his guest face the water and continue enjoying the view. The instant they settle at the table, a tall German appears, offering Farid a deferent smile. He wears a starched and stiff-looking shirt beneath a red silk vest. He waits patiently to be nodded into the conversation.

"Can I get you anything?" he says, in careful English. "Coffee? Pastries?"

"A coffee and *zwei Eier im Glas,*" Joshua says, ordering first. He makes an apologetic face for Farid, not because of his manners but because of his ordering. "That's about all the German I've got."

Farid asks for the same, and, as the man in the vest recedes, Joshua calls after him, telling him just to bring it all, the pastries and cheeses and mueslis and brown breads. "On second thought, put on a show!" he says. He does not make his apologetic face a second time. He says to Farid, "If we're eating, let's eat."

"Why not," Farid says. And, feeling it must be acknowledged, he adds, "This is very grand."

"It's too much house for me. But it's good for business. It looks like success."

"Isn't it success?"

"The accountant is the only one who can tell you that. Everything else is nonsense. Personally, I've never quite understood why a van Gogh in the boardroom of some Japanese automaker impresses anyone. It has nothing to do with how many cars they put on the road."

"I think you probably do understand," Farid says, raising a grandeur-indicating eyebrow. "I think you know just what message this house sends, or you'd save yourself a lot of money and stay at a hotel with clean sheets and Eurosport on the TV."

"I don't pick. I have a full-time fixer. She has a budget for such things, which she spends down to the last penny, because she knows if she doesn't I'll just give her less of a budget to work with the next place we set up shop."

"You need fish to catch fish. And money to draw money."

"Do you think?"

"My whole life here is built on the idea that looking a part will often see that you get it."

"What if this were a business meeting?" Joshua says. "Wouldn't you assume that the cost of heating this place in the winter and keeping it cool in the summer, that the number of people who must break their backs to keep the lawn green and the marble slippery, means I must lack some sense of scale?"

"Do you want me to agree, or to tell you, again, that I think success breeds success? To me, this house makes you seem smart for finding your way into it."

"I just think the hunger for this kind of excess is what makes the bubbles grow and then pop."

"I wish I'd met you earlier," Farid says. "I could have used that advice before the tech stocks crashed."

"You took a big hit?"

"Growing up poor, I promised never to complain when blessed with so much privilege, even when times are tight."

"I'm sure you'll make it back. Once you know how to make a fortune, it's much easier to do it the second, the third, the fourth time," Joshua says, and laughs with something like glee. "At least that's what I've been telling myself. Because it's about fifty-fifty that I'll be rebuilding from nothing by this quarter's end. I'm at that giddy spot," he says, "where I'm kind of relishing watching the whole empire burn down. I've got so much tied up in so many ventures, it's almost thrilling to wait and see which failure will drag me past the point of no return."

Farid takes another look around at the absurdity of the room in which they sit, as much to point it out to his host as to see for himself. "It can't be that bad."

"Just in time," Joshua says, waving over Farid's shoulder. "Sander rescuing me from the ugly truth."

The butler returns, carrying a tray with coffees, and toast, and a pastry basket to rival Café Einstein's. A ruddy-cheeked boy follows with a second tray, balancing a pair of champagne glasses with their soft-boiled eggs sitting inside, and a spray of bean sprouts with the most delicate follicle-like carrot shavings woven in among them, so that they look like a pair of narrow, fluted fishbowls.

When the food is served, Joshua, looking upset, first reaches into his glass and then, without apology, into Farid's. He pulls out the fancy bit of greenery and the microscopic strips of carrot and drops it all on Sander's tray.

"Tell that horrible little troll in the kitchen that I'll knock him off the box he stands on to cook if he doesn't stop making art out of my food."

The boat moves at a good clip with Joshua sitting stiffly by the tiller and Farid close by—not even daring to put a hand in his pocket lest Joshua sink them in an instant.

When all seems stable, Farid asks, "What do you want to see?"

"Besides water?"

"*From* the water?" Farid says. "We can go to Cecilienhof. That's always interesting." Joshua puts on his hapless expression, which Farid is already very familiar with, having had to walk his student through every step of every action from the instant they got on board. "It's where the Potsdam Conference took place after World War Two," Farid says. Then, in response to Joshua's unchanged expression, "You don't know it?"

"I don't know it."

"What about Glienicke Bridge?"

"Did Napoleon cross it? Does it connect Europe and Asia?"

Farid shakes his head and gives Joshua very simple coordinates, leaving him at the helm. Sometimes he corrects Joshua's steering with a word, and occasionally he reaches over and takes the tiller, turning them where they need to go.

When they reach the bridge, they lower the sails and drop anchor.

"So what is it?" Joshua says.

"This is where they exchanged the American pilot Powers for the KGB's Rudolf Abel. It was a very important moment in the Cold War. An instance of capitulation between two bitter enemies."

Joshua stays silent.

"You really haven't heard of it?" Farid says. "Never?"

"Did they trade anyone from Manitoba? Test me on something Canadian. Show me the bridge where Wayne Gretzky and Celine Dion crossed arm in arm and we'll see how I do."

2014, Limbo

There's not a soul about but for his soldiers. With the dark, and the silence, and a picture-perfect village, absent its villagers, it feels to the General as if he's moving through a dream.

As for the soulless, the bodies of those who fought back lie dead at their doors. A corpse is splayed before him as the General steps down from his jeep. The face already covered in a layer of dust from the transports kicking up clouds racing in.

It's from this place that the terrorists came, the pair who crossed the border into Israel for the prize of murdering a Jewish family in their sleep. Now the General has followed them into Jordanian territory, to extract a sort of debit on their purse.

The world had tried to head this moment off. There had been telegrams and calls and ambassadorial visits from every government that thought they had Israel's ear. The Hashemite Kingdom itself, host to these killers, was even ready to acknowledge the terribleness of such an act.

Satisfactory retributive justice was promised from the

highest levels. Glubb Pasha, the legendary leader of the feared Jordanian Legion, had personally offered to track down the attackers on home turf.

The Legion must have figured it was better to turn over their own to Israel than have the General come sniffing around off leash.

Unfortunately, the Jordanian offer did not appease. Ben-Gurion had a different sense of what was right. And so they called the General.

Always, it is to him that they turn.

His blood was already at a rolling boil as he was briefed by Ben-Gurion and Dayan and the defense minister, Lavon.

The pair of infiltrators had made their way ten kilometers into Israel. They'd sneaked into the Jewish village of Yehud, and one of the killers had pulled the pin and tossed a grenade into the house of a sleeping woman, and her sleeping children, cutting them to ribbons while they lay in their beds.

Of the woman's three children, it was the oldest boy who survived to tell the tale.

The General's first question was personal, not practical.

Where was the father? he'd wanted to know. Where was the one who should have been there, safeguarding his family?

Lavon passed a file to the General and said, "The woman's husband—the children's father—was off defending the country. He was doing his reserve duty at the time of the attack."

How this exacerbated everything for the General. A father sent off to protect the children of Israel, returning to find the country had failed to protect his own.

⋘⟨◊⟩⋙

A sloppy army, a ragtag bunch. The General has decided to clean it up, to make things nice. It is a good Russian sabra that his mother has raised.

He has formed a secret unit and trained its men. He takes a detachment of two dozen of his commandos and then borrows an even hundred from the infantry to join them on the raid. On their approach to Qibya, they fire off the mortars and light up the night.

While the shells are dropping and his troops are circling, the villagers flee Qibya through the eastern edge of town. The General has left this exit open. Let them run away so that, when the General is done, they may—like that father—return to see what he has wrought.

The General stands in the silent heart of the village, where he points at a solid stone house and says to his radio-man, "This is where we set up command."

A team races through the structure, before letting the General enter alone, a lantern in one hand, a pistol hanging from the other.

The front room is set with two elaborate divans. Through a curtained archway, he finds a kitchen, and in that kitchen is a brass *finjan*, its spout curving downward like a bird's sickled beak.

It sits atop a gas burner, lit with the tiniest blue flame, as if the knob, turned off in haste, had not made its full revolution. Someone had failed to extinguish what the General, holstering his pistol, puts out with a twist.

So sure is the General of his control of the village, he takes his time stepping back through the curtain at the sound of what turns out to be a pair of his borrowed soldiers making their way into the house.

"We have mined all the roads coming in," they tell him.

"Good, good," the General says. "And the charges?"

"They are being laid."

The General sets down his lantern and pulls the leather cover off the face of his watch. He is already unhappy with the time.

"Tell those skinny boys to work as fast as they fuck," he says. "I want fifty houses leveled. The school. The mosque. We are here to avenge, after all."

One of the two has something to say. He is smaller and fairer and jumpier than the other, who is quite dark and quite large. This fidgety one, the General dubs "the second soldier." To him, it's always evident at a glance who is the leader and who the follower in any pair. It is about spirit, not size and not even rank. It is about which, in a critical moment, would act.

It is therefore surprising to the General when it's the second who speaks up first.

"What about the villagers?" the boy says.

"What about what?" the General asks, a question for a question. He can see, even before number two answers, that his voice will be aquiver.

"To clear all those structures, sir. It will take time."

The General points out into the night. "Go fetch a jeep and make some circles. Grab yourself another useless, matchstick foot soldier to drive you around."

When the second, as is apparently his nature, looks hesitant, the General frames his mouth with both hands and tilts his head back. He is going to show them what to do. "Come out, come out wherever you are," the General calls. "This is the time for surrender!"

His head still back, his hands in place, he raises an eyebrow and catches the soldiers' gazes.

"Good then," he says. "Like that. Nothing fancy. Any who remain already know we are here."

This is the moment when they should excuse themselves and go. The first is already twisting a heel. But the second, wasting valuable time, cannot let it go. His voice turns shakier and bolder in equal measure.

"Is that enough?" the soldier says. "One circle with a jeep?"

The General studies this boy, who seems to be shrinking right in front of him. With fear in his voice—and it is not the fear of battle, it is not cowardice, but fear of the General himself—he seems suddenly so much smaller than he'd been.

"We have invaded a sovereign state for the purpose of mayhem," the General tells him. "By now, not only is Jordan mustering her troops, but battalions as far away as Iraq must be readying themselves to see how big we plan on taking this fight." The General pulls down the corners of his mouth, considering, and then his expression shifts to one of certitude as he agrees with his own assessment. "Yes, I would say if we aren't eating breakfast at home by daybreak, it means all hundred and twenty-five of us are killed."

The soldier listens, and the soldier blinks.

"Fifty houses," the General says, to this bold second. "It's you who'll decide when the job is done and when your brothers are cleared to go."

"But—" the soldier says.

The General silences him with a look. He reaches over to the first and, with a quick tug, yanks free the fresh stripes of promotion, stitched expertly to the boy's sleeve. It's nice needlework, so that the pulling leaves a giant tear.

The General can imagine this soldier eating kubbeh soup on the weekend in his pajamas, while his grandmother lovingly sews the patch onto her baby warrior's uniform shirt. All of these fighters, barely grown.

The General hands the insignia to the number two. "Now you've got a new rank, like your friend here. The others will better listen when you wave this around. You can go search for hidden villagers until your heart sits right."

"Yes, sir," the soldier says.

To the first, he says, "Set this house as well. When we leave, I want it to be nothing but dust."

The General yells for his radioman, standing right outside, pacing at the threshold. Then the General heads back to the kitchen with his lantern, lazily pulling the curtain aside just as if he were in his own home. He takes a little glass thimble from where it sits on a shelf. He pours himself the coffee, thick as oil. Even before the cup fills, the smell of sweet cardamom reaches his nose.

More than anything it is Qibya they can't forgive him, and it is Qibya that he recalls sitting in the chair in his living room, sipping from the tea that rests on the Egyptian copper tray Lily has converted into a side table.

He does the math—October now, and Qibya, it's almost exactly fourteen years ago.

Not until 1967, and the miracle of their six-day victory, did anyone dare treat him like a hero again. Fourteen years. That's how long it took for him to be welcomed back into the fold.

Forget Lazarus and his four days, the General thinks. This was a resurrection.

In Qibya, he'd razed a good part of the village.

From Qibya, he'd returned without losing a man.

Then the call came from Lavon. Not congratulations from the defense minister. Not kudos on a successful mission—the riskiest, boldest ever pulled off by their fledgling state. All he heard through the phone was, "What have you done?"

A massacre, is what Lavon said. Women and children. And again the refrain, "What have you done?"

The General finds Lily out brushing the horses. She feeds her favorite apples and carrots while the General explains.

"It appears" is the phrase the General uses to tell his wife. "It appears the Arabs were hiding in the houses. Women and children," he says, "as the saying goes."

"All women and children?"

"Among the dead there were many. The Arabs always inflate the numbers, but they're saying sixty-nine all told. The full count."

"It's tragic," she says. "This bloody, endless tit for tat."

"It is," says her husband. "It is."

Ben-Gurion almost immediately denied it—denied *him*—to the press. The old man told the world, "Vigilantes! It was our poor Jews of Arab Lands, our Holocaust survivors. They live on our borders and suffer attacks without end. What can I do? They take matters into their own hands. An uprising gotten out of hand."

The General knew it would sound as ridiculous to the world as it sounded to him. Angry Israeli civilians with mortars and mines? Angry Israeli villagers crossing into Jordan in darkness, carrying enough explosives to level a village made of stone? A foolish lie. How could the old man not think in the moment how such a claim might play out?

Ben-Gurion summons him to his home in Sde Boker, for a visit in the desert. He invites the General into his simple quarters, where he sits on his single bed, monkish in the way of so many founders of nations. The prime minister wears an undershirt and short pants. He's managed to cross his legs beneath him, a limber old Buddha.

Ben-Gurion says, "Tell me. Tell me what went on that night."

The General says nothing. And the prime minister climbs off the bed and, slipping into his sandals, says, "Let's walk."

The General understands immediately. It is easier to discuss some things facing forward than when looking each other in the eye.

They wander out to the very edge of the desert in silence and stand side by side on a cliff overlooking the great barrens. The old man says, "This is where my grave will be. Picture what the Negev will look like a century from now. Picture standing at my marker and everything before you in bloom."

The General stares out over the wadis and the tabletop mountains, setting his gaze on the vast blue sky. He keeps his focus there and guides the old man through the mission, explaining how they breached the defenses around the village itself, and how they first fired upon Qibya and, also, the next village over, a place called Budrus to the south.

The General explains his way to the house in which he set up command, and where he drank the coffee, still hot, from the *finjan* on the stove.

He knows the old man wants operational analysis, the tactical details laid out.

What the General tells him right then is about the ancient phonograph. How he'd dispatched the two soldiers and called his radioman in.

And there it was, against the wall in its wooden case, holding pride of place.

He tells the old man that, even in the moment, he was shocked to think how easily one can miss something right before his very eyes.

The General had his radioman crank it up. And the first thing they heard was the needle scratching itself dull at the record's empty center, the speaker playing the sound of no sound.

He relays to Ben-Gurion how he told the radioman to go raise up the lid and move the needle. Everything from the General's mouth, an order.

He had said, "Let us hear the last song this house ever played."

They stood there, he tells Ben-Gurion, listening, in Arabic, to the most beautiful voice in the world.

That's when the sappers began returning, rolling out their wire on the spools, the wheels turning, the men bent and backing away from their targets, as if prostrate with respect for the destruction to come. And all during this, the General standing in the doorway, the album playing, and— with the convoy revving up—that voice faintly heard.

That is when the first soldier came running up along with part of the General's demolition team.

The old man, listening closely, says to the General, "The first?"

"There was a pair. First and second. The first had a tear in his shirt. I'd instructed him earlier to come back and prep the house."

He'd watched, the General had, as explosives were set around that living room at a satisfying rate. Yes. He'd trained them up well.

The General re-cranked the phonograph and then, waiting by the entrance, stepped aside as the last charge was drilled into the doorpost where the children's heights were marked. When the song was over, the speaker hissed, all crackle and heartbeat, the needle pushing against an empty groove. "Right then," he tells the old man, "I gave the signal. The radioman radioed, and the last of us mounted the jeeps and trucks and rumbled off."

The General turns to the old man, who stares out into the desert.

"That's when we blew Qibya to the ground."

The General leans back in his chair in his living room, and he thinks about that record. More than any of the spoils of any war, it was that album he wishes he'd carried home.

It's that beautiful voice he hears right then, as if it were singing directly into his ears. First the voice and then the not-voice that replaces it, the needle turning against silence, living beyond the last groove.

This stretch of quiet, the General knows, would soon be pierced by that crack rolling across the fields. The waiting makes his chest go tight.

While the quiet is still his, he recalls what the old man had said to him. He remembers and he observes as, right before him, Ben-Gurion takes a deep, dry breath of that hot desert air. He watches as the old man turns his back on the view and begins his trek toward the kibbutz with its low-slung buildings and its walkways lined with patchy, burnt grass.

The General follows, devoted, at his heels.

As if passing judgment, as if sharing a terrible truth, the old man says, "You are our bulldog. You know that, yes?"

The old man turns to see what his protégé might say in response. The General, catching up, walking at the old man's side, answers with the same silence that now runs, a simultaneous loop, in his head.

"I still can't tell if having you will be for this nation a blessing or a curse. Not since bar Kokhba came popping out of his tunnels to bloody the Romans have we had one man who can do so much harm."

"A nation needs to defend itself."

"It does, doesn't it," the old man says.

They consider this as they stroll back to Ben-Gurion's quarters.

At his door, he says, "The world hates us, and always has. They kill us, and always will. But you, you raise up the price," the old man tells him. "Don't stop. Don't stop until our neighbors get the message. Don't stop until killing a Jew becomes too expensive for even the rich and profligate man. That is your whole purpose on this earth," Ben-Gurion says. "You, put here solely to raise the bounty hung on the Jewish head. Make it expensive. Make it a rare and fine delicacy for those with a taste for Jewish blood."

2014, Black Site (Negev Desert)

It's amazing what skills one can master given enough time to perfect them. Prisoner Z sits up in bed, in the dark, the stack of magazines on his lap as a desk, writing. Over the years, on the nights he cannot sleep, which are legion, Prisoner Z has not only greatly improved his penmanship in both Hebrew and English, but has become adept at composing without any light. It's easier than one would think.

He is busy writing a letter to the General, his pen pal. In the morning he will give it to the guard, to give to his mother, to give to the General, who never writes back.

It's the only avenue by which a prisoner-unnamed, in a cell-unlisted, might plead his case-that's-not-a-case. The thrust of his letters has changed over time. Prisoner Z is no longer requesting to be freed, to be exonerated, to be sent to the States, so much as he is asking, only, to be made into a person again—an actual detainee, entered into a system that might see him properly pay for his crimes. He is inquiring most politely, wondering if his being might be returned.

Sometimes the content of these letters is legally bent,

sometimes political, and, though the guard has limited Prisoner Z to one sheet per missive, sometimes they are much more expository and personal in tone. It's a tricky thing trying to touch the heart of a man who has, toward you, been only heartless. Hard to personalize yourself to the person who has seen you undone.

Feeling it out, hoping to connect, he is hoping to stress only this:

"We are birds of a feather, me and you," he writes the General. "How many times did you do what you needed to save Israel? Against all accepted wisdom. Against all advice. Misrepresenting your intentions. In defiance of our, and everyone's, laws.

"You did what you needed to rescue the people even when they didn't know they needed to be saved.

"We are the same, you and I.

"To lose this war with the Palestinians, to cede ground, to raise the white flag of surrender—it is the only way for us to win. History will prove it. Only now, the history for which I fight is, as yet, the future unknown."

And when writing to the man responsible for his erasure, Prisoner Z very well understands he should act erased. A writer must know his audience, is his position. And so on all these letters to the General, he always signs, as he signs right now,

Most Sincerely Yours,
Prisoner Z

2002, Berlin

The wind on the lake picks up, and the boat rocks beneath the Glienicke Bridge. Farid, who sometimes drinks on the water, his one exception, is having a beer plucked from the cornucopia that is the picnic basket sent along by Joshua's household staff.

They'd dropped anchor and drifted until the line went taut, yet Joshua sits frozen on the deck, his knuckles white around the tiller, as if he's still steering. Farid thinks his friend looks a little green.

"You know, you can't get seasick on a lake. It's almost impossible. Or, maybe it's completely so."

Joshua smiles a weak smile.

"Sorry. That's what my girlfriend calls my misery face. I don't have much of a filter," Joshua says, very obviously attempting to perk up. "Do I really look seasick?"

Farid tells him that he does.

"Just suffering," Joshua says. "But not from the water. It's more a personal sort of queasiness."

"Is it trouble with that girlfriend?"

"I should be so lucky. It's work. And it's exactly what I

came out here to forget. Look at this nice bridge! So distracting and full of history."

Farid laughs at that.

"That's why I sail," Farid says. "These lakes are the only place I calm down."

"Sadly, it seems my problems also float."

"Well?" Farid says, offering the opening his companion clearly seeks.

"I don't want to complain."

Farid opens another beer and, before passing it, reaches over and physically removes Joshua's hand from the bar.

"You're complaining already. What you're not doing is being specific about why."

"Fair enough," Joshua says, raising his beer in a half-hearted toast. "One of our big deals is going sour. I've basically been printing money since I started this company, and now I think maybe I'm in over my head. I never should have switched to computers."

Farid takes a perfect apple from the basket and sits on the deck opposite, stretching his feet out into the cockpit.

"What were you doing before?"

"It's what you said at dinner, about your father and boring business? I may have made the single dullest fortune in the world. I got rich off sand."

"Seriously?"

"Very much so. Construction aggregate. Industrial and recreational. Pretty sand to rebuild the dunes and beaches everyone pretends aren't washing away. Sand for playgrounds and horse arenas. In L.A., we supplied to movies and TV. We sold mountains of the stuff for mixing into concrete. Fascinating, I know."

"So how do you get from sand to computers?"

"I didn't. I went to metals. Aluminum, and then nickel,

which took me to Russia, where it became very obvious, very quickly, that I really was in way over my head. And here I am, working in computers, and ready to crash again."

"It's too late for that. Everyone underwater with computers already drowned last year. Myself included."

Some schoolchildren up by the foot of the bridge wave and scream until Joshua and Farid pay them mind. When the two men wave back, the kids erupt and fairly burst from ecstasy.

"You're talking dot-com stuff," Joshua says. "It's the sexy side of the industry that tanked. As I told you, I don't do sexy. I sell refurbished hardware."

"You must sell a lot of it then."

The comment seems to cheer Joshua, as if reminding him of the savvy part of what he does.

"Do you know how many machines a single large company turns over in a year? They flip about a third of their inventory. Desktops, laptops. For someplace with fifty or sixty thousand employees, that's twenty thousand computers. Obviously, those are the dream contracts. So divide that by ten. If you find a business with six thousand people, of which there are endless in North America, that's two thousand units, and the companies are happy to have someone haul it all away. To pay them for the privilege, they take as a boon. I fix everything up, good as new, then ship it abroad."

Farid stares out over the water. He is already running the idea through his businessman's head.

"How much of it is salvageable?"

"You wouldn't believe the mismanagement at these places. Some of it has never come out of the boxes. And of what does, I'd say upwards of forty percent of what we get is A-grade. Another twenty is a solid B. The rest, I strip for parts."

"And it's all corporate?"

"I won't touch the universities. They use everything to death. I do have a guy in New Jersey who gets me the old U.S. government computers. They come without the hard drives, which makes the margins worse, though people are tickled to have them. Where I do enormous volume is in cell phones. There's maybe five years left before they'll be so cheap, people will just toss them. But now, they're gold."

"Can I ask the numbers? How does a regular deal break down?"

"Don't be shy!" Joshua says.

"I live like a German, but I think Palestinian. We are not a reserved people."

"With the laptops, I can fit a thousand in a container. My markup?" Joshua says, and signals to Farid that he'd better hold on to something so he doesn't fall out of the boat. "Embarrassing as it is to admit, I net between five and seven hundred percent, depending."

"What does that translate to?"

"With laptops, or flat-screen monitors, I pocket two hundred thousand." Joshua tips his bottle back to his mouth and drains his beer. Farid thinks it's to hide his obvious pride.

"That is a tremendous profit, for what sounds like not too much work."

"Yes, at this point it's basically a couple of e-mails on each end. When things were running smoothly, that came out to a hundred thousand dollars every time I hit send."

"So what's the problem with the most perfect business model I've ever heard?"

"The more I ship to a place, the more I eat into the profits of the folk getting rich off new machines. My model works no matter what, theirs doesn't if all those teenagers aren't crying for the new phone, the new computer, the new everything every season. They don't want 'refurbished' to become too attractive a term. People need to believe their electronics are all outdated after six months."

"So how do they stop you?"

"In this case? It's easy. It's Egypt. Someone who doesn't like me knows someone and made a call, and now I've got about a zillion dollars' worth of phones stuck at port. Five forty-footers filled with Nokias and Motorolas. And I have another five containers on a cargo ship that, unlike this boat, I can't turn around. I assume, sitting here on your beautiful wooden yacht, that you understand how liquidity works."

Farid sees the way his friend is looking at him. And Farid laughs, this time more deeply, and with a sincere knee slap, because it's all so offensive and all so good. He stands up and takes hold of the winch. He can't believe he didn't see it coming.

"Here you are," he says, "with a new Arab confidant who does import-export, who may also just have contacts in Egypt, and the whole time you act like talking business is the last thing on your mind."

"I promise, it's not because you're an Arab."

"It never is. And I'm sorry to disappoint, but I can't do the magical *baksheesh* trick and get your merchandise out for you."

"Did I ask you that? I haven't treated you with disrespect," Joshua says, looking honestly wounded.

"It's the disrespected one who gets to decide that."

"Trust me, I was just looking for a break and some time on the water. I wasn't being coy and I don't do business like that. I don't expect you to believe me, but I want you to know, I do appreciate this day. Anyway, I should probably get back to my castle and start working the phones."

Farid obliges, sailing them back quickly and in silence. It's as they pull into their slip at the marina, and weighed down by some adopted Germanic sense of comportment, that Farid says he could take Joshua out again next week.

"Only if you let me tack and jibe," Joshua says, chipper. "Only if I can prove that I've learned."

2002, Paris

She stays the night and the next day, and then stays on for another. She tells Z she has roommates in an apartment not even fit for one. There is only a standing shower. She has a very uncomfortable bed.

She tells him this to make clear that he shouldn't take her staying as a compliment. It isn't him. It is that deep, giant tub.

She takes long baths, and then, after running out for supplies, she takes them with bubbles, and after the bubbles, she starts taking them with him.

She goes home on the third day for some clothes and better shoes. This is also when she starts grilling him over his very strange hermetic life. "I'm an out-of-work waitress," she says. "A professional bohemian. You have no excuse for living in Paris and hiding at home. Also, when you think I don't see, you make a face that looks like you're going to die."

"Problems," is what he tells her. "I have problems that I'm trying to solve."

"Should I be worried?"

"They aren't contagious. They're troubles of the ethical sort."

"You have ethical troubles?"

"It's more that I *don't* have ethical troubles. What it is, is I got myself into a bind trying to fix the world."

"That sounds mad."

"Okay," he says.

"Like *pazzo*-mad. Like, insane. It does not sound like what you say if you're well."

"Okay," he says, again.

"You're not going to tell me? With us all cozy, and me practically living here, doing whatever it is we are doing together?" She stares at Z, and he stands there, resolute, as if, no, he isn't going to say.

"Fine!" she says, studying the man before her, deducing. "This isn't a drug dealer's house. Of that I'm sure. Even a bad one lives better than this. And I know you're not in the Mafia, because I know what that looks like too." She squints and takes a spin around the apartment, before settling in front of him once more. "You're not running weapons."

"You can tell that from the apartment?"

"Yes," she says. "Because I once dated a man who sold submarines. You should have seen what his house looked like."

"You dated a man who sold submarines?"

"That is not the issue right now. The issue is you, being loving, and kind, and looking secretly miserable, and hiding out. If we're supposed to be falling in love—are we supposed to be falling in love?"

"Yes," he says.

"All right. Then I want to know, right now, what it is you do."

Z goes to talk, and before he utters a word, she, with her hands on her hips and her lips pursed, shakes her head.

"No," the waitress says. She's not having it. "I can see already that I'm going to get nonsense. I want the truth. If you're going to trust me, trust me now, or I go. I learned this lesson with the submarine man, too late."

Z already can't picture being without her. Not just out of love, but at the thought of facing a loneliness that was often greater than the fear.

Oh, how he has been dying to tell her. Oh, how nice it would feel. He could cry just imagining the relief.

Z takes a deep breath. The waitress, taking it to be a sincere action, relaxes her body and drops her hands.

"It's what I think it is, then?" she says.

"What do you think?"

"It really is crazier than I first thought," she says. "Right? There's only one thing I can guess in a house with no personal details of any kind, and a man who tells me only stories from when he was young. You're a spy? Yes?"

"Sort of," is Z's unsatisfactory answer.

"Sort of?"

"The term. It really gets misused." And trying to appease her, Z says, "I mean, colloquially."

"So you're a smart spy, who cares about grammar?"

"To me, a spy is more someone who spies against his or her own country. I'd never do that. That's treasonous. Or, it's the wrong kind of treasonous."

"Is there a right kind?"

"I'm saying, it's wrong. But that some wrong things, in certain circumstances, are inherently right."

"But you are a spy?"

"I'm an operative. More or less."

"For who?"

"For *whom*?"

"You're very annoying for someone asking a great amount of understanding from the new woman in his life."

"Sorry. Precision, when I'm under stress. I know it's an issue."

"It's annoying."

"You said, and I apologized."

The waitress puts her hands back on her hips, she taps a foot, and she considers Z, in his new, spy-ish form.

"It still sounds crazy," she says. "But it also makes some sense." Then, at least fleetingly passing judgment in his favor, Z thinks, she kisses him for a good, long while.

2014, Jerusalem

The Shabbat siren sounds, and Ruthi yells at her secular son to turn off the TV. "Go stream nonsense on your computer in the bedroom," she says, "and put on a shirt with buttons for dinner."

Ruthi lights the candles on the tiny patch of open counter next to the sink. The table, they carry back and forth to the balcony, depending on the height of the sun in the summer and the rain in its season. So she does her lighting in the kitchen, as, during the Sabbath, the candlesticks are not to be moved.

Ruthi waves her hands before the flames and then presses them to her eyes for the blessing. It is in this window where a mother's wishes are made.

She first prays for her son's good health and good fortune. Then she prays for the General. Let him find his way back. Let him finish what he started. Let him return to lead this country to safety and final borders, and a peace that will usher them into the future, even as the countries around them burn. She adds a prayer for the poor children of those countries, and one for the parents who shield them. On and on her wishing goes, until she stops herself, circling back to her son, so as not to over-wish her weekly allowance while welcoming the Sabbath into her home.

It may be the first time in his life that the General can sit in his den and read the paper in peace and quiet, but for that shot, like the player's needle endlessly spinning.

That sound, it never seems to go away.

The General heaves himself up, as if the air raid sirens were suddenly screaming, dumping the bowls in his lap to the floor. The General runs outside, taking the path behind the burn barrel, his dogs darting after him in a lather.

He runs the dusty track to the front gate, hanging ajar, and races out into the road. He stands in its center, not yet sweating in the heat, his system still catching up with the mad dash he has made. The General cries out, screaming his son's name. He calls to the boy, though the boy is right there. His son, his legacy, the one for whom he fights all his battles, the one for whom he fought them, even before this child was born.

Here he lies with a bullet to the head, and next to him the General's prized rifle.

The ivory stock is covered in dust and wet with blood, and still the General can see, it's a treasure. Two treasures, he thinks, as he scoops up—and runs off with—his wounded and dying and already dead son.

He knows, right then, for a father to survive this is unthinkable. For him to live even one second after gathering up what cannot be, something is not right. The General holds the boy's bloody body close and he looks, carefully, around. Yes. Something in his universe has gone awry.

2002, Berlin

Farid takes the last tie and finishes flaking the mainsail. It is a beautiful evening, and he is in no rush at all.

Joshua waits for him on the dock.

"I liked that a lot, today," Joshua says. "I'm feeling more confident, if that counts for anything."

"That's a big part of it. Also, you sail better late in the day."

"Maybe it's you noticing fewer mistakes when it's darker."

"Or it could be that."

When all is trim and neat, Farid accepts a hand from Joshua and hops out of the boat. "I do think some people do better at certain times of day—in all things. If you're a night person, you should recognize that and do what's most important when you're most at ease."

"Life lessons and sailing lessons," Joshua says.

"I'm not kidding. It took me a long time to learn that."

Joshua nods and, already holding his keys, starts to walk off. He stops when Farid doesn't follow.

"I'm going to stay," Farid says.

"I figured you might." And, as if it needs explaining,

Joshua says, "I mean, that first week, I saw you here. Just, you know, watching." When Farid says nothing in reply, Joshua waves goodbye, keys jangling, and heads toward the path to the street.

Farid watches him, calculating, trying to get a read.

Surprising himself, he calls to Joshua, feeling as he does so that he's speaking way too loudly. Then, though he'd really thought he'd wait on a different opportunity, he says, "I wanted to ask you. What if Egypt wasn't your worry anymore?"

"What if what?" Joshua says.

Farid's question pulls him right back.

"I reached out to some people about your Cairo deal. If you're interested, I know a person who can solve your problem at port."

Joshua raises his hands in surrender.

"Honestly, I wasn't trying to involve you. I'm still embarrassed I brought it up. It's been bothering me ever since," Joshua says. "Anyway, it's way too big a favor to ask."

"I wasn't offering a favor. I was making a pitch."

Joshua keeps trying to wave the whole thing away. "I couldn't bear dragging you into this mess. Even if you helped clear Customs, they'll shut us out of the market. It's a nightmare, no matter what."

"Which is, again, why I want to discuss it. What if Egypt wasn't your nightmare anymore? If your figures are anywhere near what you say—"

"They are," Joshua says.

"Then let me be your representative for merchandising there. You won't have to bear the cost of inventory. I'll pay based on the volumes you move."

"I don't understand."

"Exactly," Farid says. "You don't understand. But I do.

I have connections, powerful people, who really like the terms I brought them. Also, it's not about Egypt for me. I want Gaza as a territory too."

"That sounds like even more of a nightmare than Egypt," Joshua says. "No offense! Or, if it's too late for that, what I'm trying to say is, I thought there's a blockade on?"

"Which is why my offer is so good. I'm making it so that these aren't your worries. And if it works with the small stuff, then you and I can discuss going big. The utilities in Gaza, the sewage treatment, the power grid, it's all been knocked out by the Israelis. We could do servers. There is no limit once we start."

"That is big."

"There is a lot at stake, for a lot of people."

"Does that mean I'll be breaking Israeli law?"

"Israel's laws aren't the world's. And they definitely aren't Palestine's."

Again, Joshua concedes defeat. "Let's not go there. I'm asking, how will you get merchandise through if the borders are closed?"

Farid shakes his head, disappointed in Joshua's ignorance.

He points down, and Joshua looks down.

"Underneath," Farid says. "The same way everything gets into Gaza. Through the tunnels."

Joshua does some nervous foot tapping and, finally, wipes his nose on the back of his hand.

"It does sound like you've got it covered," he says. "And I need it covered."

"Is that a deal?"

"It could be. Only, it's not how I do business."

"Obviously, we'll set written conditions. I'm not asking to do it on a handshake."

"It's not your end I'm worried about. It's mine. If we're going to do this," Joshua says, "I want you to send someone to my guy in Cairo. He has a couple of laptops and a whole mess of phones. I want to know that you really can get things into Gaza. And, before we start, I want you to know that everything is as tip-top as I'm promising."

"Even better," Farid says.

"Listen, I'll get you the info before I fly to Mumbai on Wednesday. I'm back the Wednesday after. Talk to me then," Joshua says, and puts a hand on Farid's arm. "If it all still sounds good, we can draft some contracts. But first, I want to hear that you're happy. It's important that when you look at me you see the face of a man you can trust."

2014, Hospital (near Tel Aviv)

Poised as the night nurse is, on the outer edge of the crush of people assembled around the General's bed, it's she—looking absolutely guilty—who is first to catch Ruthi's eye.

The doctors are in the room along with a team of nurses, and, because the General is an important man and a legendary figure, and because he is himself a bulldozer who raised a pair of bulldozers for sons, it seems that the family could not be convinced to lessen its swelling numbers.

Stuffed in with the night nurse and the attendant hospital staff are those two sons and their wives, and their many children, whom Ruthi can't help but count, even then, confirming that all the General's grandchildren are in attendance.

She has not even crossed the threshold when the night nurse hooks her arm and takes her back into the hall.

"It happened right after Shabbat. The sons already here when I showed up." She frees Ruthi's arm so that she can turn her friend to face her, now grasping Ruthi's shoulders firmly. "They made me promise. I obviously wanted to call. I was dialing already when they stopped me."

"None of that matters now," Ruthi says, though it deeply and painfully does. If she could have, she'd already have killed the weekend aide—from the rotating cast of ne'er-do-wells, none of whom Ruthi trusted—who'd covered her shifts when she was home. "Only tell me," Ruthi says, "what's gone wrong?"

"Everything. Whatever little was working isn't anymore. First the lungs, then the heart, now the kidneys are going into failure, and the liver is on its way too." She pauses to *tsk-tsk* the medical facts of it. "From the liver, it's never long."

Dr. Brodie exits the room then, pushing past without a word. The extraordinary power that the doctor carries away with him draws the family's attentions outward, where they see their sweet Ruthi coming apart (she is well aware) in the hall.

They fawn all over her. From their manner, it would seem to any observer that Ruthi is also family, and that it is true tenderness and warmth that she receives.

Rightly so. For not only has Ruthi been caregiver to an incapacitated father and grandfather, but for how long prior was she his beloved and loyal right hand? Back in those days, Ruthi was like another sibling to those sons and daughters-in-law: attendant at the family gatherings, in on the private jokes, unfailingly available to listen to, absorb, and allay their endless worries about a sizable, excitable man who was always stretched perilously thin.

When the General was newly prime minister, and Lily still newly gone, Ruthi was like another grandmother, as well. She remembered the birthdays, spoiled the kids rotten, filling in wherever possible for the General's love—always great and plentiful when he had time to give it—while he ran a country that was never not on the edge of destruction.

The skinny son now hooks her arm, as the night nurse had, and escorts her over to the bedside. The littlest grandchild hangs off her free hand.

Ruthi knows and keeps telling herself that the family's tenderness is genuine, troubled as she is by the knowledge that the choice not to call her was equally sincere. She struggles to focus on the General while abashedly reconciling these contradictions in her mind.

Ruthi leans over the side rail and, freeing her hands, presses them hard to the General's, feeling him, still with them, alive.

She stays there for no more than an instant before letting go and backing silently out into the hall. Because *like* family is not family.

After all those years, Ruthi sees herself as no more than what she definitively is, an employee hired to do a job. Looking in upon that vigil, she watches the circle close up around the bed, the General hidden from view.

2002, Paris

They wake up twisted in the sheets. It is late in the day and Z and the waitress are both confused for a moment as to where they are. The waitress tells Z to get dressed, she's going to treat him to a fancy dinner, a thank-you for all his generous hosting, since she basically moved in on their first date.

When Z says that he doesn't want any thanks and, anyway, he'd rather eat in, the waitress won't hear of it.

"You go out when you want to. You must. I met you out twice."

"Lapses in judgment," he says. "Both times."

If Z won't budge, the waitress says she's going to make him a nice *heimishe*-Italian meal. She will see to it that he is thanked whether he likes it or not. "If you didn't adore me before," she says, "you will after I cook."

The waitress goes downstairs and returns loaded with groceries. Along with the food, she's also bought him a pair of proper wineglasses and two very fine bottles of wine. "Open the white," she tells him, "while I get to work."

She pokes through his cabinets, making do with the poor

selection of pots and pans and the one passable broken-handled cutting knife.

"I'm impressed," he says, as she moves confidently about, stopping only to pass him her glass when it needs topping off.

"This is nothing. A nice, easy pasta. A salad, so your Ashkenazi heart keeps pumping."

"You're already worried about my health?"

"From the instant you told me you crossed the city for chopped liver three weeks in a row."

It's all moving along seamlessly but for the salt, which he doesn't seem to have, and which she finds to be an astonishing testament to his sad bachelorhood. "Salt, olive oil," she says. "These are basic things."

She grabs his keys without asking and nips out to the corner store.

He looks out the window when she goes, following her down the block in that gloamy evening light.

The dinner they share is as simple and homey and wonderful as the waitress promised. She grates bottarga atop his spaghetti, and, like all things related to this woman, when he tastes it, he falls instantly in love.

"It's my father's favorite," she tells him. When he asks her exactly what it is, she says it's better just to eat and enjoy.

Z does just that. Eating and enjoying while gazing across at a person whose giant curls fall perfectly into her face every time she looks down at her plate.

When he tries to pour out the end of that second bottle of wine, it's the first he senses how long they've been sitting and talking and drinking, and how fully besotted he is.

Z has barely lifted the bottle when the waitress stays his hand. "An unmarried man should never pour out the last drops."

"Are you sure about that? I'd be shocked if there was a superstition we didn't have in my house."

"This one is Italian, not Jewish," she says, and she works so hard to empty the bottle, Z expects she'll wring it out like a dish towel before she's done.

They take their glasses over to the sofa, which is set against the short wall between dining table and bedroom that, in Z's rental, passes as a salon. The waitress sits with her back against the sofa's arm, and her legs stretched across Z's lap.

"I can't believe you're in my apartment," he says. "The beautiful waitress who brought me my lunch. And—if it's not too creepy?" Z says, waiting for approval to potentially creep her out.

The waitress nods, magnanimous.

"When I walked into the restaurant you were at that front window, facing the street. I was already smitten before you turned around. Is that too weird to admit—the falling-for-your-back bit?"

"For my back? That's the part of me you fell for?"

"It was all of you," he says. "All your parts, fallen for equally."

"I'm sure," the waitress says, with a raised eyebrow and a good long drink of her wine. Then, remembering something, she sits up and swings her legs off Z's lap. "Oh my God!" she says. "Speaking of . . ."

"Of your parts?"

"Of the restaurant. There was another new waiter trying out that day."

"Yes," Z says, his blood pressure—at mention of that waiter—already on the rise.

"You remember him?"

"I do, actually. I did not like the look of that guy."

"Right?" she says. "Something was off with him. He kept saying he had a lot of experience, but he couldn't balance a tray." The waitress switches to a conspiratorial whisper. "I don't think he'd waited tables before."

"I guess he didn't impress. Because he never came back either. They must have fired him after his audition too."

"The opposite. He's the one who turned them down. I was so much better, and they offered him the job."

"How do you know? I thought you both only worked the one shift?"

"That's what I'm trying to tell you. When I went to get the salt, I forgot to say. I bumped into that waiter."

"You bumped into the Huguenot?" Z says. "Like a big, mean-looking waiter—a giant, handsome, mean-looking gay waiter? With sort of blondish hair, and an unnaturally strong chin. Like, maybe there is a horseshoe stuffed in there."

"You don't need to describe him," she says. "That's who we were already talking about."

"I was confirming that we meant the same person," Z says, really, really needing her to confirm that the man she just saw was, for sure, the same one he meant.

"Yes, of course, it was him. And yes, he is very handsome—even more handsome with that chin. It fits his face well."

"Very handsome," Z says. "And you're saying he was also at the store?"

"He was on the corner, here, having a chat with that vagrant who always sits on the end of your block."

"The bum? On the suitcase? They were chatting?"

"Yes," she says. "And you know what?"

"No," Z says. He does not know what. Not at all.

"He was very friendly today. You would think he was a different person from how he was at the restaurant. So cocky."

"But was it a different person?"

"No. It was him." The waitress fetches her phone from the table and hands it to Z. "He gave me his number and said we should get a drink."

Z can feel his face twisting up, so distressing is her report.

"It isn't like that," the waitress says, standing over him. "It was so clearly friendly. He wasn't starting. I promise you, he's not interested that way."

"Did you tell him you saw me?" Z hands her back the phone without even looking.

"Did I tell him that I was having dinner with a man from a table that he didn't serve, from the place he worked for one day? No, I did not."

"He remembers me, I promise. He saw me come in. I saw him see me! He made a call."

"Yes, I'm sure your lunch meant a lot. I'm sure he was downstairs because he wants to thank you for eating in his presence. A great honor."

"It's not funny. I need to know, did he say anything about me at all?"

"You're serious? Is he supposed to be a spy too? Is he your enemy, the waiter that you never met?"

"I am life-and-death serious."

"This is why I never date the Jewish men. Not because there are too few in Rome. It's because of this. Because of how you act right now. You all seem very cute for a day or two, and then end up being crazy. Crazy mama's boys, every last one. It's the Gentile girls that get raised thinking you make good husbands."

"I'm really sorry," Z says. "I'll calm down," he says, without calming at all. "Just tell me what he said, exactly. I wasn't kidding about the trouble I'm in."

She looks at him with hooded eyes and sits back down next to him, but, he notes, they no longer touch. The waitress reports the rest to Z, somewhat jokingly, though he can tell she is giving an accurate account.

"He said hello. He said, *'Tiens, quelle surprise!'* Or maybe I said that—"

"Who said it?"

"Him," the waitress says, reflecting. "Then I asked what he was doing around here. And he said, meeting a friend for a movie. Then he asked me—"

"Exactly what did he ask, and how did he ask it?"

"That's what I'm telling you. He asked me if I lived here. I told him, no. I told him that I was having dinner with a friend—a friend who has no salt. Then I showed him the salt, because I didn't take a bag at the shop, and the salt was in my hand, and because I guess I thought that it would be funny to present it right then."

"That's it?"

The waitress sighs, exasperated.

"He told me his friend lives on this block too. Then he asked me what building I was going to, because maybe it was the same one."

"Was it?"

"It was. But on the other side."

"At the back, the-other-side? Or the opposite entrance, at the front?"

"The front," she says. "The other front stairs."

"How do you know?"

"Seriously? I know because I told him I was in the front but on this side, when he asked me."

"And you answered?"

"Is it a secret? He doesn't even know I'm with you."

"It kind of, sort of, was."

Z gets up and starts pacing, because this somehow feels like it will help him think. "Where is he now?"

"Now? I assume not where I left him."

"I'm saying, which way did he go?"

"No way. He went to his friend's. They're probably in some hot French movie theater watching balloons float across the screen."

Z stops, frozen.

"He picked up his friend? In this building? Did he get buzzed up?"

"Of course not. I let him in. I just told you that we were going to the same place."

Z shakes his head, fully disappointed. In her. In himself. His mind then split between dark scenarios unfurling at lightning speed, as well as a slow-motion remorse as he remembers the waitress picking up his keys on her way out for salt. He has added himself to the image so that, in recalling, he is also looking down upon his own dumb, doting smile.

He can see from the waitress's own pitched-browed, wide-eyed response that she, in a non-teasing way, really thinks that he's maybe mad as a hatter.

He will fix that later, if he can. But he's already in the bedroom, grabbing a leather satchel in which he drops his favorite of the books he's bought. He stuffs in a Patagonia shell from the pile of clothes in the bottom of the cabinet, and he does all this very self-consciously—as the waitress, now leaning back against the deep solid archway that separates the rooms, gawks at his frantic running around.

Z sticks a hand under the mattress and pulls out a flip

knife. It is a large and stupid-looking thing that he bought from a cutlery stand at the open-air market, a table set with cheese slicers and nail clippers and faux-hinged steak knives that don't really fold, as well as a few implements of violence.

Z opens the knife with one hand, and, looking over at the waitress, he can see that she's not the least bit afraid of him, even like this. Her trust touches him deeply and is also disheartening, for making clear how absolutely un-terrifying a man he seems.

Z passes her by and grabs a chair that he takes over to the bathroom. He steps up and works the knife blade into the top edge of the flimsy bathroom door, prying off the strip of wood between the panels.

With that strip popped loose, Z holds the knife in his teeth and, hand over hand, pulls up a string that hangs in the narrow hollow.

Attached to the end of the string is a ziploc bag, sealed with packing tape. He hops down and heads to the dining table to cut it open.

Inside are a passport and three fat stacks of bills, two in euros and one in dollars, rubber bands stretched around.

"Good," the waitress says. "That's an improvement."

"What?" Z says, his face tight, a sweaty seriousness about him.

"Now you seem less crazy, and more like a dangerous spy."

"Do I really seem more dangerous?"

"Not really. I was trying to be nice because it seems like it matters to you."

"It does. If I were a bit more threatening now, it would help."

"To scare the waiter who has come to kill you?"

"Yes, because of him."

"You still don't seem very scary. But you do seem legitimate. The passport and the money, they make you seem authentic. But shouldn't you have maybe five passports, or a gun?"

"The passport thing is only in the movies, and the gun for a different kind of spy. If the French came in here to arrest me, how guilty do I look with a half dozen identities lying around? How do you talk your way out of that?"

"How do you explain a passport inside a door?"

"One is odd, the other is criminal."

"Well, either way, I'm much more likely to believe whatever it is you're about to tell me you're caught up in."

"And you?" Z says, as he breaks up the money. Some in each pocket, some in the leather bag. He gets on his knees and pulls another ziploc from where it's taped under the couch.

"And me, what?"

"Are you caught up in it too?" he says, standing.

"You think, because we spent the week together? Because we had sex and took some baths and I made you dinner and bought salt?"

"Sort of, because of all that, yes. Because I think, new as it is—we have something good."

"So, what you said before, it's the opposite. Your troubles are contagious. And now, because I've been exposed, it's like I have a kind of espionage-STD? That doesn't make much sense."

"You could go home."

"Will I get home?"

"I bet you will. I bet it will be fine."

"You 'bet'?"

"You're linked to me now, and, unfortunately, you're also now marked in some way."

" 'Marked'?" she says, looking rattled for the first time. "I don't like that at all."

"I'm just saying, it would make sense to keep tabs on you. But you haven't done anything. They will see that you're innocent and a waste of resources."

"When will they see that?"

Z stands there, trying to wait her out, to be patient, but things are feeling really pressing. The Huguenot, if he's still in the building, has had ample time to prepare whatever terribleness he's been sent to deliver. Every extra instant is in the waiter's favor.

"I need to go somewhere," Z says, "to a hotel, or a hostel, or something. Even just for a night. Just until I can figure out a next step. But it has to happen now."

"And you want me to join?"

"I want you to do whatever you want."

"If I do go home, and forget about you, you promise I'm not going to end up getting tortured? I don't want to be dunked in water and made to talk. That's a nightmare I've had since I was a little girl."

"I'd be very surprised if that happened."

"You're quite the salesman," she says.

"Then, I promise," he says. "It won't happen. You'll be safe. Your roommates will be safe. I'm sorry if I said it wrong."

The waitress purses her lips, first aiming them left and then right, her perfect nose wrinkling in the sexiest of concerned manners.

"This is the moment, traditionally," Z says, "where you decide if you're on board."

The waitress thinks about this and taps at that broken tooth with a fingernail, as if she's checking to see if it's grown back on its own.

"Well, if I come along. Where do we go?"

"Pretty much anywhere that's not here."

Giving that tooth three more thoughtful taps, the waitress lowers her hand and says, "If I do come?"

"Yes?"

"I don't do hostels. There's only so much sacrifice I can make, even for adventure."

"You can pick the place."

"And you're really not going to get me killed?"

"And not dunked in water either. If we get out of here, absolutely not. If they don't have to surprise us and can see, in public, that we are two, it will be fine. It's very clear that who wants to talk to me wants only me."

"To talk to you?"

"To capture me, to torture me, to maybe kill me if options one and two aren't feasible."

"One more thing, then, before my first-ever escape. Answer that and I'll join you."

"Like in a fable."

"Sort of."

Z straightens his back, shakes out his arms, and nods.

"I'm ready. Ask away."

"This is really more to make my father happy. It's how he raised me. But still, even to rebellious, sleeping-with-strangers, socialist me, I admit, it matters."

"I can respect that."

"So tell me, operative. Is what you're doing good for the Jews?"

2014, Limbo

Oh, how it torments him, the sound of that shot. The General practically leaps from his chair.

He drops the newspaper on the side table. But the paper keeps dropping. The table isn't there.

The General finds it behind him, beneath Lily's weaving, pushed up against the wall. Atop it, in place of the tea he was drinking, sits a small clay menorah, caked with wax. It is wonderfully misshapen, with pencil-bored wells spaced too closely together, ready for the candles that will burn too quick. A masterpiece one of his grandchildren made in school.

This makes the General smile, doubly so, as he spies, between the feet of the table, the crumpled foil from a chocolate coin.

He can't understand why the menorah is still out, the floor still unswept, all the way to October, almost a year after the holiday fell.

And if the calendar really stands at 1967, then who are these grandchildren he already loves, so far from being ushered into this world?

It is not right, the General knows. It has been, for some time, not right.

The General does not run to the road to find his ghost of a son. He does not call for Lily, already gone. He will look for a mirror, is what he decides. For it cannot be both present and past, and the General wants to see which face he wears. He wants to know if he is old or if he's young.

On his way to the foyer, where the closest mirror stands, the General pinches himself—hard. He feels the pinch and feels sure that he's not dreaming.

He follows the pinch with a deep, deep breath, and he knows too that this must mean he is not, himself, yet dead.

But that shot, then, how can it keep on shooting?

None of it makes any sense. Unless, unless.

The front hall mirror is covered with a sheet, as if the General inhabits a house of mourning. He wiggles his toes and looks down at his feet. He's not surprised to find himself padding around in socks, as if newly bereaved.

Nobody wants that, the General thinks. And the General closes his eyes tight-tight.

Reopening them, the General is relieved. Yes, he must have been dozing. It is the simplest explanation—for he is seated again, the copper tray table that Lily made back at his side. On it stands his mug of mint tea, the steam twisting off in a wisp.

Cautiously, the General lowers his gaze to his lap to find that the two bowls are where the two bowls belong. A comfort, followed immediately by another. His dear Lily—he has been calling for her—peers out from the kitchen, a towel in her hand.

The General wants to ask her what is amiss. But then there is the sound of the shot—distracting.

Leaning back, the General says aloud to himself (for he

knows, already, his dear Lily will not answer), "Maybe it is that I am not well."

He is a legendary strategist, the General. He has always been able to see the best way out, even in the midst of chaos.

Quagmire after quagmire, failure atop failure, with all his repeated ruinations and unravelings, the General has managed to reach all the way to the office of prime minister. Him! With all that blood on his hands.

Yes, the General knows this to be true. He is their leader. He knows too this must mean he's already old.

This must mean he has already given up Gaza. This must mean he is busy planning for a Palestinian state. These decisions, he knows he has made them and that they fly in the face of all he'd ever believed.

He takes particular interest in these concessions. Look at how his aged self is able to wield compromise as a new brutality. If he's come to those conclusions it can mean only one thing. This must mean there's some trickery behind it. He must somewhere believe it's the only way to win the Palestinians' ruthless, fecund, demographic war.

The General flexes his stiffening fingers. He rolls his stiff shoulders. He tries on his now-creaky old self for size. It is not bad, this body, rickety as it is. And it fits so well, in his equally rickety, form-fitting old chair.

This taking of stock, he finds it pleasing and so reflects upon a long life lived. He remembers his way back to boyhood and finds himself in short pants under the Tel Aviv sun. He stands in his mother's yard as she walks toward him with a cluster of purple grapes held aloft. He can feel himself reaching.

He fights his way forward, through the endless battles, military and political. He forges on until he hears it, not the shot but a different sound, like a wave crashing down. He hears the great rush of voices as the people chant his name. He has been crowned King of Israel, their savior. The General stands tall on the Temple Mount, bathed in this rallying call. He cannot see their faces, shielded by a phalanx, a show of strength.

He is letting his people know that however painful the sacrifices he will ask—this place, hallowed ground, he will never surrender. Not the jewel of their unified, undividable city.

To the edge of that thought is as far as the General's mind will go.

2002, Paris

They do not exit through the door but climb out the bedroom window onto the little sloped roof of the caretaker's shed. The waitress does not hesitate as they shimmy down on their bottoms toward the eaves.

"Does anything rattle you?" Z whispers, astonished by the waitress's alacrity and calm.

"If the roof was higher, maybe," she says. She then turns around and, slipping down over the edge, hangs for a moment before dropping the couple of feet to the ground.

Z passes her the bag and joins her with a quiet thud. She helps him up, and while Z dusts himself off he peers toward the darkened archway at the front of the building.

Seeing no one, he swings the bag over his shoulder and leads the waitress past the rear entrances, and beneath the second arch, beyond which stands a neglected garden, its trellis affixed to the perimeter wall.

"This was actually once a road," Z says of the cobbled path beneath their feet. "It was the first that ran directly from the river to the Sorbonne. That's why the front entry is so wide."

"A perfect time for a tour."

"A relevant time," he says.

Z kneels down, as if he is going to propose, and, inter-locking fingers, he offers her his linked hands as a step.

They hop the wall and find themselves on the continu-ation of that path, in a courtyard that mirrors the one they just left. They pass under the archways and at the other building's front gate they press the button to release it, step-ping out onto the street.

"You rented an apartment with its own escape route?"

"I did," Z says. "It's not so paranoid when you use it to do just that."

Ready to bolt, Z takes hold of the waitress's wrist. She pulls it free and takes hold of his.

"Fair enough," he says. And feeling like he maybe, just maybe, might survive this night, he takes off with her on a happy sprint over to the main thoroughfare and across the first bridge, where they meld into the nighttime crowd out-side Notre-Dame. At Rue de Rivoli they slow their pace and step into a taxi waiting at a light.

They sit there quietly, and the driver looks to them, prop-erly annoyed.

"Your call," Z says to the waitress. "As promised."

The waitress leans her head toward the space between the seats and asks for the Hôtel de Crillon.

"Are you kidding?" Z says. "That's the fanciest hotel in the city."

"My thought exactly. No one is going to be looking for you there."

The waitress takes charge, putting Z at a table in the high-flown lobby so she can go check them in. He has questions that she shows no interest in hearing. All she wants to know is if Z wants to be awake or asleep. And when he doesn't understand, she says, "Coffee or alcohol?"

He opts for the former, and the waitress orders him an espresso and a champagne for herself. She goes off to get them a room with a confidence that truly surprises.

Z maps the lobby, looking for pattern and broken pattern, for aberrancy and awkwardness, for sturdy shoes whose quality is at odds with the suit above, for greetings overly performative, for meaningful eye contact between strangers, for furtive checkings of phones or a nervous glance at a watch. He hunts the employee in one sort of uniform inexplicably manning the wrong station.

In the midst of this, lit with hyperarousal and at his fight-or-flight best, Z sees the waitress throw her head back and laugh. He hears the sound of her laughter from across the room as their drinks arrive.

Feeling a kind of ease, Z sips his coffee and eats the micro-sized heart-shaped cookie plucked off the side of his saucer. He forces himself to savor it, even though it tastes as if it were made of some elegant mix of pistachios and butter, rosewater and sand. He tells himself—maybe the least harmful deception of late—that it is a treat.

As the waitress comes happily his way, he thinks fate should have switched their roles. She is gifted at compartmentalizing and looks more natural on the run than he does. She sits in the ridiculous bergère chair across the table. She knocks back her champagne, and, standing, leaves a few coins. "They'll put it on the room," she says. "Now let's go hide in style."

"Holy shit," is what Z says. He's never seen anything like it. The sitting room is extraordinarily grand, as is the view out onto Place de la Concorde.

"It's like being on a honeymoon," he says.

"Yes, a honeymoon where someone is also trying to kill you."

"Like that, exactly," Z says. He opens the door to the bedroom and says, "Holy shit," a second time. As there is no bedroom, but a staircase leading to it.

"Come up here," he calls. "This is unreal."

The waitress joins him, taking it all in stride.

"Yes," she says. "It's very nice."

"We can't pay for this," he says. "I can't. You can't."

"I can," she says. "That is, my father can and already is. It's on his card. And, please," she says, putting up a hand as Z tenses, "don't start with the paranoia about him being linked to me and then me to you. I told them not to put through any charges until we leave." The waitress goes over to the window and pulls aside the curtains. "My family, we stay here all the time."

"All the time?"

"Since I was little."

"I thought you were sharing a tiny place with too many roommates. Remember? No tub!"

"I am."

"For sport?"

"To build character."

"So you're super-rich, then?"

"The super-rich find the 'super' part unpleasant to admit. It's not polite."

"But you are?"

"Do you think I'd have come along if I wasn't? This is

not a poor girl's escapade. It's for someone who does not worry about having very big problems be made to go away. Anyway, have you ever heard the average Italian speak English? Listen to me," she says, of her fluency. "Growing up in Rome, English like mine does not come cheap. You're the one who works in intelligence. These are some very obvious signals to miss."

Z agrees with her, both aloud and to himself. He thinks again that they should really swap places. The waitress is so much better at all of this than him.

2002, Berlin

Joshua slaps at the night table, hunting the clock, then feels his way around the wall above the headboard, searching for the switch that sets the sconces over the bed alight.

"What time is it?" he says into the phone, now for the second time, and still without reply.

He knows Farid is the night caller, and that Farid has been holding his silence for an inordinately long stretch, breathing heavily down the line.

Joshua believes the breathing to be a kind of soft cry, a noise he could not imagine coming from this man.

"What time is it?" he says again as he collects himself, though at this point, he can see the clock flashing 3:55.

"You are the new one," Farid says.

"I don't understand," Joshua tells him. "I am the new what? What's going on?"

"You. You are new. It's not a collaborator on the ground. Not a drone in the sky. It's only you."

"What is not a drone in the sky? I don't understand, Farid."

"Tonight, all of this, it's a godsend, for you, yes? An

added bonus beyond the strike? All of us trying to figure it out together. Everyone talking without thinking. All that new chatter for you to sift through, so you can better map relationships, better string the pictures together, moving all the tacked photos around on your boards."

"What boards, Farid? I don't understand."

"It is sloppy behavior on all our parts, I know. But a leak this big must be patched. There is someone inside, the only option anyone can figure. As everything is perfectly secure on the Gaza end. Then it hits me—here in Berlin, a world away from the fighting. I am the one. I am the weak link. It's all too neat and all too convenient, for you to suddenly arrive."

"What's happened?" Joshua says. "You need to tell me."

"Even now, you continue."

"Honestly, it's four in the morning. I'm not continuing anything. I was asleep."

"A massacre, Joshua."

"I don't understand," Joshua says, his voice gone high, and sweating already in his bed.

"In Gaza they are pulling bodies from the rubble while the houses still burn. You hit your target. You killed my brother. Good for you, Joshua. You made him a martyr, which we can always accept. It is the children, Joshua. The building next door. The whole family dead. What have you done?"

"What are you saying, friend? We are in Berlin. I am in Berlin."

"The Israelis dropped a bomb on my brother's building. Only, when they leveled it, they leveled the one next door too."

"Please," Joshua says, his heart racing. "Take a deep breath," he says.

He requests this of Farid but is really only trying to command it of himself. The panic—he is so bad with the panic, the panic is beginning to bubble and stir.

"There's no one," Farid says. "No one new in our circle. Nothing new on the ground. Nothing has changed in Gaza, nothing in Damascus, nothing in Beirut. No one can come up with anything, until—"

"Until what, Farid?"

"Until I come up with you. It's the phones, isn't it! You show up with your business. You show up with free money, just when we need. Computers when we need. And I take them. I take your fucking refurbished phones. And I get them to my people in Gaza. And now my brother, and all those near him, are dead."

"Oh my God," Joshua says, rushing to process. "You don't really think—"

"What I don't think is that I can get over that gate. If I thought I could make it in there to strangle you myself, I would."

"Please, friend, what are you saying? I, honestly, don't understand."

"How much better would this day be if I also afforded you the excuse to shoot me dead on your front lawn?"

"No one wants to shoot you, Farid."

"Still, for this, for what you have done, we will have our revenge. Already, the streets of Gaza are filled with mourners. Already the people march. Turn on your TV. Find the news. You will see. A river of people five kilometers long."

"But I had nothing to do with it."

"Don't embarrass yourself any further. This is a courtesy call from your enemy. I just wanted to let you know, the economy of terror only strengthens. For the children you have just taken, we will take from yours. That's what I wanted to tell you, Joshua. There is a price to be paid. You have, tonight, just murdered your own."

"Now wait, Farid," Joshua says. "Don't say such a terrible thing."

"What is terrible to a Canadian? What does a sailor from Toronto care about Jews and Arabs around the world."

"Of course I care," Joshua says. "Children are children. Whatever you're saying, whatever you're threatening—"

"No one is threatening," Farid says. "This is not about what we want to do, this is not about a plan to be made. I am calling so that you understand, what has already been put into motion did not have to happen. What already cannot be stopped was started because of this, because of you."

Joshua, who knows he should say nothing, who has been trained not to say a word, feels a deviant sort of urge to reply. It's as if he's somehow ended up on the wrong side of all the bulwarks and firewalls and partitions put in place to keep him from feeling, for Farid, an actual, human emotion.

He makes a split-second decision. He says, "We didn't start this fight."

"But you did."

"Whatever you're going to do, I beg you, please—a sensible man. Let's talk this out."

"Whatever I am going to do is already done."

2014, Limbo

Hauling himself from the chair, the General folds the newspaper along its creases and places it, along with the bowls from his lap, on the tray, next to his tea. The sound of the shot, it pulls him. But he resists running toward it. Instead the General drives himself back to that mirror, where he tears off the sheet.

What he finds for a reflection is his prime-ministerial self, and his mighty-warrior self, and his wounded-soldier bleeding-out self, licking his lips and dying of thirst. There in that mirror is his smiling, purple-smeared, grape-faced, short-pantsed self, whom the General is tickled to be.

This iteration, built of iterations, fascinates the General more than it unsettles. He calls excitedly to his wife in the kitchen. He wants to catalog for her all these odd ruptures and twists in time.

The General calls to Lily. But Lily does not come.

He has never been without responsibility, never moved without purpose, and knows to this task too he must now urgently attend. He coolly and methodically tries to make sense.

He thinks it absurd to posit that he is in Heaven, simply because he ends up in his beloved chair, on his beloved farm, time and time again.

Equally illogical is to assume that he is in Hell, solely because of the sound of that shot and what he knows, racing toward it, he will find.

Where is he then, he wonders, where time leaks the way it does, crossing and uncrossing, where a moment plays in an endless loop? He knows he is not dead, but this cannot be a life.

And then he wonders, could it be some in-between place? A threshold from which to wait. A kind of Sheol, a limbo space, from where he could not, without his own approval, move on. There is precedent, of course. There have been, haunting this realm, other Israeli kings.

The General laughs at that, an uproarious belly laugh. He has always said it—as a sign of confidence; to intimidate and threaten and cow—and maybe it has finally come to pass. Maybe it is all over, but nothing can kill him until he lets it. The General, stronger than death.

Considering this last option, he lowers his newspaper and raises up his head from where he sits, relaxing. He has an article he's been meaning to finish and his tea to drink. He could stay here forever. If not for the shot, he might contentedly sit in that chair for all time.

"Come, come," the General tells himself. For him, a man of action, to sit static for eternity. No, it is not a proper everlasting for a man of change.

But how to remedy it? The tactician, yet again, finds himself fully taxed.

The General looks to the empty brackets on the wall, the rifle gone. And he thinks, for such a job, of the curved

Caucasian dagger in its sheath that sits in a shadow box atop his desk. It was a bar mitzvah gift from his father. A gift and also a responsibility. A bestowal at maturity, meant to signal what direction his life was expected to take. The others got fountain pens, and for him—smart boy, well-behaved boy, newly minted man—from his father he is given a weapon of war.

He does not move to go get it. He cannot slit his own throat, he is aware. Not because of cowardice, of which he truly has none. It is because the General, though never a religious man, lives by Jewish principles. It is against all he has ever believed to take his own life.

It would follow, then, that moving on from this place must defy physical action. The change, he hypothesizes, must come through an effort of mind.

What if it were no more of an effort than waking oneself from a dream? The same quick, messy struggle, but with an opposite exertion, wrestling his way toward a deeper, darker sleep.

And here it comes again, the laughter! Who would have thought that it would be with laughter that the General goes? To him it is funny to have to try so hard. How many had given their all to be the one to kill him? How many times had he given everything he had, simply to hold on?

The General takes a last, deep breath. He shoulders that ancient and legendary drive, forcing what he knew as himself the other way. He settles back into his chair, and hears the shot, and runs to the road. He flies through the air with his radioman by his side and plants his feet atop the Temple Mount—a colossus. It is deafening now as the multitudes cheer him on, chanting "General, General, King of Israel!"

He basks in the adulation. And from somewhere over it, he can just make out, in Arabic, the sound of that plaintive song.

Ruthi stands over him, though he cannot see it. It is night, the broader family gone from the room, the mothers home tucking in children, the two sons standing outside the building in the always-perfect weather discussing what is to come. The night nurse, who was sound asleep in the corner, jarred by Ruthi, is already mumbling herself awake.

Ruthi hovers over the General's bed, pressing and pressing the call button and crying out, her voice rolling down the hall.

One of the useless schoolboy doctors is on night shift. He comes groggy from his cot, fast-walking down the corridor because doctors do not run. A pair of staff nurses trail him, and when they enter, Ruthi points to the General and says, "Look!"

The night nurse is up now, holding her cell phone in her hand, ready to summon the sons back to the room.

While Ruthi points, demanding of the physician that he do whatever it takes, all in attendance now look at her like she's a madwoman. The doctor, rubbing at his eyes with the back of his hand, says, "There is no change."

"He is dying," Ruthi says. "It is happening now."

She can tell from how they gawk at her. "How embarrassing," "How pitiful" is what they all think.

As that baby doctor opens his mouth to placate Ruthi, to tell her to calm herself down, it is not the General but all his machines that suddenly wake up.

There are bells and whistles. There is a gaudy show of

flashing numbers and spiking line, like a jackpot struck. The room awash with all that terrible information.

In the split second where thoughts turn to deed, all look to Ruthi.

Somehow, she'd caught it.

This woman. Astounding. How could she know?

2014, Black Site (Negev Desert)

It's always worse after the weekends, with Prisoner Z acting hurt and abandoned, and the guard, feeling high-spirited and refreshed after some time at home, returning to face his prisoner and be reminded of how trapped they both are.

And now, it's all that much harder.

The guard sets up the backgammon board on Prisoner Z's bed, and Prisoner Z, starting right in on him, says, "You're acting weird again. And don't tell me you're not. It's been a solid week straight."

"You're projecting," the guard says. "Because this place has made you insane, and you try and put it on me."

Prisoner Z tilts his head and gives the guard his best stink-eyed look. He's not buying it. He shrugs and goes over to his shelf. He pulls the letter he's written the General from where it juts out of the pile of magazines.

He hands it to the guard, who puts it straight into his bag and, without looking up, shakes a die, tossing it to see who rolls first.

The guard throws a five, and Prisoner Z throws a six. But Prisoner Z, on the edge of the bed, sits still.

The guard, staring at the board so that he doesn't have to look at Prisoner Z, holds out until he's fully frustrated and then says, almost yelling, "There's only one move to make. It's a standard opening. I've seen you make it thousands of times."

"Do you know how many times I've made it, exactly?"

"Please don't freak me out with your crazy math," the guard says, looking up. "Please, don't tell me you remember exactly how many times you've had a six-five."

"Nope, I don't," Prisoner Z says. "But I can tell you that the score is now 21,797 to 24,446. You're making great strides. I have less than a three-thousand-game lead."

Prisoner Z presses his eyes closed and, opening them, says, "If we play like seven and a quarter games a day, you could catch up in a year. But you'd have to win them all."

"It's terrifying when you do that."

"All I'm saying is, it would be great to be tied again. I love it when we're even."

"It's your obsession with being even that put you in here in the first place. Nothing is even. The world, that way, is not fair."

Prisoner Z does not like this at all. Not the answer, and not the peculiar mode in which the guard is talking.

"You're being philosophical," Prisoner Z says. "Or your dum-dum's version of it. And you can't tell me I'm making it up. You only reflect in here when things are dire."

Prisoner Z is stunned at the response he receives. He was poking about but did not expect to strike a chord.

The guard's color drains, and Prisoner Z thinks, if someone walked in on them, they'd have trouble guessing who had last seen the light of day.

He reaches into his bag and takes out Prisoner Z's letter. He places it on the board, between them.

"I've been trying to tell you," the guard says. "There has been a development."

"In my case? With this extraordinary miscarriage of justice?"

"Sort of," the guard says. "It's about the General."

"Did he finally answer one of my letters? Is that why you're giving this one back?"

"He's dead," the guard says. "He died."

"Who died?" Prisoner Z says, his tone completely flat.

"The General."

"That would be something," Prisoner Z says, and he closes those eyes again, trying to picture it.

"It is something. It's happened."

"Then tell me which of his endless enemies finally put a bullet in his big fat head? Was the assassin domestic or imported? Arab or Jew? I really can't guess."

"Not killed, just dead," the guard says. "I'm not kidding. He passed away Sunday."

Prisoner Z is staring at the guard, blank.

"This one?"

"The one before. It's taken me a few days to get the courage up."

This, it is a lot to process for Prisoner Z. It sounds like the guard is saying that the General, the one who locked him up and erased him, the only one who could bring him back into being and free him, is no longer.

"I don't believe you," Prisoner Z says, not wanting to believe.

The guard stays silent, which is its own sort of reply.

"Then what did he die of, if he's dead and no one killed him?"

"Technically?"

"Why 'technically'?"

"He died of complications of a stroke."

"He had a stroke? How do you not tell me that the only one who knows I'm here had a stroke?"

"I'm telling you now."

"Well, when did he have it?"

"Earlier."

"What are you saying? Was it in the papers? Did regular people know? Or is this something your mother told you during pillow talk?"

"Fuck you," the guard says. "And, yes, the stroke was in the papers."

"Fuck," Prisoner Z says. "Fuck, fuck." Then, with his eyes full of water, and looking right at the guard, intimate, "When?"

"When was the article?"

"The stroke. When did he have the stroke?"

Here the guard gets up and, in a very Prisoner Z–like way, paces nervously in the cell. When the guard stops, he has his eyes down to the floor and scratches at a spot that isn't there with his toe.

Prisoner Z has never seen anything like this from him before. A completely new action he's never cataloged in all these years.

Again, Prisoner Z asks, "When did he have this stroke?"

The guard steels himself. He looks into the prisoner's eyes with real love. He'd honestly just been trying to protect him.

"In 2005. Late December, I'd guess. Really, the big one, it was 2006. It sort of all happened right before and right after Sylvester."

"What?"

"Eight years ago. The big one, right after the New Year."

"I don't understand."

"I didn't think you would."

"I mean, you're kidding me," Prisoner Z says. "You have to be kidding."

"He's been in a coma."

"The General has been living in a coma."

"Sort of."

"In a coma?"

"Sort of living. Since 2006."

"And you didn't tell me?"

"I didn't want to upset you."

"The only one outside this prison who knows I'm here has a stroke. The one person in charge of my fate—my freedom—has a stroke and you don't say anything for nine years?"

"Eight."

"What?"

"Eight years."

"Fuck! How could you keep that from me?"

"My mother and I. Well, more my mother. She prays. And she was hopeful. For his sake. For yours."

"What are you saying?"

"I'm saying we were hoping, the two of us, and really, when you get down to it also the nation! We were all hoping, together, that one day the General—maybe he would just wake up."

2002, Berlin

Joshua sits in the sunroom, overlooking the lake. He bounces a leg and wipes the sleep from his eyes.

The kitchen door opens, and in comes the boy with two coffees on a tray. He hurries to serve and hurries away. Before the kitchen door closes behind him, Sander is already pushing through the formal entrance, his silk vest undone and, yet more shocking, his crisp shirt unbuttoned beneath that vest.

Joshua can see Sander's tanned and hairy stomach right out there in the open. He turns to the wall of windows, through which anyone with a pair of binoculars might see this break with decorum.

Sander follows Joshua's gaze and seems to understand his concern, and also not to care.

He drops down in the chair next to Joshua's and picks up one of the coffees. Taking a boiling sip, he says, "Shit," and then, "Shit, that's hot."

He blows atop the tiny cup with what Joshua can only acknowledge is a mighty exhalation and takes another sip. "Have you ever heard of anyone getting burned on an espresso after it's already made its way to the table? Jesus," Sander says, "that kid." And then, squinting his eyes as if uncovering the conspiratorial, "Is there some way to turn up the boiler on those machines? Can you make it extra hot on purpose?"

"I don't think so," Joshua says, listening nervously. For he cannot quite grasp how Sander, his reserved and stoic and generally silent German house manager, seems to have switched from speaking English to Hebrew.

"Then that little shit must have run it in here just to spite me. He's the most dangerous character under this roof, and the only one who's not supposed to mean any harm. Even that evil little chef does his job without incident."

"I don't understand," Joshua says, stressing the English.

He's doing his best to catch his breath, though it hasn't, since the phone call, fully returned. He looks out the windows again, this time at a racing shell passing nearby. He focuses hard on it, trying to mine the calm from all those oars breaking the water with an even grace.

"You don't understand what?" Sander says, fully committed to the Hebrew. "Is it the point I'm making that's confusing, or the words themselves?"

"Please, Sander," Joshua says, practically begging. He knows the boy who brought the coffee can hear this in the kitchen. "I really don't understand."

"Is that all you have in your fucking arsenal?" Sander says. Then, twisting his face up, mocking Joshua, he employs a tone that Joshua finds to be unfairly whiny. " 'What? What? Who is this? I don't understand!' "

Edging into a full-on panic, Joshua slides into Hebrew himself, pleading for Sander to quiet himself down. "What if the boy hears?"

Sander shakes his head, as if there were someone else there besides Joshua, to register his disappointment. "That was the boy's last coffee. He's already gone. What you need to worry about is how we fix the mess that you made. What if the Germans were listening? What if the Americans, who listen to the Germans, were listening to them listening to us? The sirens may already be headed this way. And that's without considering what happens if Hamas wants to fight it out right here. You, with your big mouth, have fucked us good."

Joshua presses at his chin with his palm, rotating it until his neck gives an audible crack. "What even happened over there? They're talking about a massacre on every channel. There are pictures of people carrying dead children over their heads."

"Yes," Sander says. "Evidently, our target was hiding in a taller building that tipped over onto a smaller building, where there was an unrelated family. A large family, judging by the reports."

Joshua turns pale. He can feel the tips of his fingers tingling, as if he might pass out. "So then, it's really us who did that? We just killed a houseful of children?"

"It's not us. It's that the larger building fell funny. It's gravity behind that. Gravity unforeseen."

Sander then scratches at his hairy chest, and Joshua takes note of how powerful a man he is. It does not show, all that muscle under his clothes.

"A baby girl," Joshua says. "Two months old."

"What do you want me to tell you? It's twenty of our kids on purpose, or ten of theirs by accident. No one forced our target to dispatch a stream of killers. No one made him make bombs."

"We just dropped a one-ton bomb onto a slum. We used a fucking fighter jet to strike inside our own borders. It's not even an enemy state."

"No, no, no. That's where you get it wrong. Palestine isn't a state when it concerns statehood. When it comes to warring, it's a state, yes? The Palestinians, they live in a country for the purpose of war."

"Do you know how insane that sounds?"

"And do you know how many Israelis have been killed in the last week? The last month? Because I do. I know by heart. When you're worried about the unlucky people killed today, think of the five Israelis killed last week in Tel Aviv, and the nine killed the day before them in Emmanuel, and the seven killed the month before that on French Hill, and the nineteen blown up less than a day prior in Gilo, and the seventeen blown up on a bus in Megiddo the week before. And that's only June. All of those attacks facilitated by that one man. And those same attacks were all financed by, and likely plotted with, his brother, your friend."

"He is my friend. He was. We should still use him. If Farid can plan these things, he can also unplan them."

"You're finished with Farid. And probably with the Mossad. We'll see what the fallout is from blowing your own cover on that call."

"But he knew. He figured it out. He said it was me and those phones."

"He can say what he wants, you didn't need to confirm it. I cannot tell you the ramifications of that slip, they reach far beyond the mission to which we were assigned."

"I'm the problem? I'm the fuckup here—because of that call? What about what we just made happen, you and I? What about that murdered family?" Joshua, as if absorbing what he's said only after saying it, drops his face in his hands and lets out a moan. He looks back to Sander, who is unfazed. "I thought I was selling computers," Joshua says. "I thought I was opening a pipeline so we could listen in. It would have been a dream, that kind of access."

"*You?* No, *you* are not selling anything, or opening anything. You are just an idiot, who screwed up a simple, simple conversation. It was Joshua. Joshua was selling the computers. He was the one on the job."

"Yes?" Joshua says.

"Joshua, for you, is done."

Joshua doesn't dare say that he doesn't understand. As a workaround, he goes with "I am trying to grasp," which seems to enrage Sander in exactly the same way.

Taking the arms of Joshua's chair, Sander turns it from the table, pulling it forcefully, the chair's feet shrieking against the tile.

Sander does not release his grip, even when the two are facing each other, knee to knee.

"Listen carefully," he says, bringing his face close, as if to aid comprehension. "For you, Joshua is *gornisht.* The Gaza deal is *gornisht.* Berlin itself is *gornisht.* And, depending on how these next hours go, the Mossad is maybe *gornisht* for us both."

"Like that? For one single slip?"

"Yes. For one treaty-breaching, illegal-action-on-foreign-soil-stating, possibly Geneva-Convention-violating admission of a slip. Now, you need to run upstairs and get me Joshua's passport and the international license and the business cards right away. Go get me everything with his name written on it. You don't want to miss your train." Before Joshua can ask, Sander says, "We've got you on the seven forty-six out of Hauptbahnhof, switching at Hannover and then at Karlsruhe. If you make it, and if you're lucky, you'll be back in Paris by tonight, as if none of this ever happened. Tomorrow morning, you'll be at your old front, selling printer paper and mouse pads to the Iranians all day. The people of Tel Aviv will again be able to rest easy."

"How can it have been worth blowing the operation for one man? We could have kept it going. They'd have bought everything. Printers, scanners, laptops, copy machines. We could have been completely tapped in. Total access to all communication," Joshua says. "I've only just finished the first part of the deal!"

"This, we've been over," Sander says, impatient. "Someone else is already Joshua this morning. Someone better and smarter and much more dangerous than you. I'm sure he'd have loved to explain it all himself. Unfortunately, Joshua had to run. He has some pressing business to attend to in Shanghai." Sander looks at his watch. "By now, he's already boarded his flight at Tegel and is busy telling the person stuck next to him all about what Joshua does."

"And you?"

"Which me?" Sander says.

"Any you."

"I'm still belligerent, bossy, Hebrew-speaking Sander for about an hour. I'm sorry you won't be here to watch me finish molting. To see what bird I turn into next."

"And Farid?"

"Don't trouble yourself. Farid is already someone else's headache. And don't be fooled by the man you met. He's as bad as his brother. The only difference is Farid fights from a yacht."

He does think that he is beginning to understand what Sander-who-is-Sander-for-but-one-more-hour has just told him. He understands that Farid is the enemy. He understands that Joshua is right now buckled into his seat and taking off on a plane.

Thinking hard, he also understands that, while he slept, he'd participated in something violent, and terrible, and deadly. And that, with one slip of the tongue, he'd turned back into himself.

"You should feel good," Sander says. "The General feels good. He has already released a statement to the news. You fucked up, but you're also a hero. This was a hugely valuable mission, target-wise. So if your exit goes smoothly, tomorrow you'll be balanced on your hemorrhoids in Paris, making cold calls, and saving the Jews."

"How do I go back? After this? What we just did—it's not what I signed up for."

"Actually, if you think about it even for a nanosecond, it kind of, exactly, is. It's just what you signed up for."

"I signed up to prevent violence. To disrupt technological advances that will lead to war. To collect data—harmless data, by selling our adversaries the machines that will catch it. I joined up to gather intelligence from our enemies."

"And what the fuck do you think we do with the intelligence you gather?"

Sander then reaches behind and brings forward a manila envelope bent, the long way, in half. "Here are your tickets, and a replacement passport, fresh from the embassy—still warm as toast."

Z accepts the envelope. Z accepts what has just transpired. He opens the cover to the passport to see who he will be for his return to France. He flips through the visas and exit and entry stamps.

While he does so, Sander gets up and goes over to the wall, where he presses down on a large metal toggle. With the grinding hum of some ancient engine, the shades in front of Z's beautiful view slowly draw down.

"That's it?" Z says. "We're just done?"

"The moment that bomb hit, we were done. It's your indiscretion that has also made our decamping a bit of a rush." Sander, staring out at the lake as the shades cut into his outlook, sighs deeply. "Prepare as we might in this business, we don't work in a sterile field. Always we must be ready for change. Now go upstairs and get your things sorted. In the meantime, I'll make you a peanut butter sandwich and cut some cucumber for the train."

"You're packing me lunch?"

"That is Plan A. If you hurry down with your bag, and the things I asked for. If not, I switch to Plan B. And instead of the sandwich, I will knock you over the head and drag you into the kitchen, where I will, with great speed, chop you into pieces and feed you into the industrial food processor. Then I will spend the morning waving at the neighbors over the back hedge as I pour you, bucket after bucket, around the gardens and into the lake for all the happy little fish to eat."

2014, Black Site (Negev Desert)

"Take it," the guard says, calling in from the hallway. "It's point-two-five milligrams. If you were free, you could still operate a backhoe after. It's just to cut the edge."

From the looks of it, it would seem that Prisoner Z is not currently interested in having any edge removed. He stands on the bed, yelling down at the guard through the peek-a-boo window in the cell door.

Prisoner Z is having a very reasonable breakdown, considering the news. The guard, expecting as much, had already fetched a feel-good pill and now takes turns reaching his hand through the slot, offering the capsule resting in his palm, and trying to speak sense to Prisoner Z through it.

"Sister-fucker! Son of a whore!" is what Prisoner Z yells. "Let your guard down—guard—and I'll split your head like a sunflower seed! Come in so I can show you from where the fish pees!"

"A classic," the guard says, admiring, while also respecting the gravity of the situation.

"Deep breaths," he says to Prisoner Z. "You need to slow down your heart."

Prisoner Z appears to process this last bit. He takes some deep breaths, eventually climbing down from his bed.

Looking petulant, in the guard's opinion, Prisoner Z approaches the slot, opening his mouth and sticking out his tongue.

This time, when the guard puts his hand through, Prisoner Z accepts the capsule. He steps back so the guard can see its gelatin jacket stuck to the end of his tongue, and then, like that, he swallows.

2002, Karlsruhe

Z dials from a pay phone at the Karlsruhe station, while waiting on his connecting train. He can't believe it when Farid answers, and he says, "I thought you'd already have gone to ground."

"And miss a chance to talk to you and whoever else is on the line?"

"It's only me this morning. The others are busy scrubbing away fingerprints and pulling up stakes. We should probably talk quickly. I can't promise they won't be listening again soon."

"Let me guess. This is the call where you try and turn me—on the day you killed my brother? Is that what your recruitment manual recommends?"

"No. It's not recruitment. If anything, I'm calling to turn myself."

A soft laughter comes from Farid, hardly different from the sound of the crying that Z had heard during the four a.m. talk.

"I'm serious," Z says. "I'm bringing you a second deal."

"From a man whose face I can trust?"

"I want to help level the scales."

"And how will you do that, Joshua? Because I already have my own plan for the same."

"I can get you things, Farid. Useful things. I have access."

"You're going to compromise your side, because you feel guilty?"

"I'm going to protect my side by trying to fix an imbalance that cannot and should not be maintained."

"So what is my part in this?"

"Your part is no part. I will get you what you need to protect your people. All I ask is that you do nothing in return. End the cycle. That's how I'll protect mine."

Farid takes a moment, and Z listens to the sound of a train rolling off.

"Call me after," is what Farid says. "Let's finish this round first."

"Please," Z says. "Don't do it. Whatever it is, just see what I get you before. See the lengths to which I'll go. Give me a couple of days. You can give me that long."

"After," Farid says. "Talk to me then. If you're going to murder our children, you must be prepared to drink from the same cup of poison."

2002, Paris

Z tells her about those sweet and pure years in Jerusalem, the Peace Process years. He tells the waitress how wonderful it felt to live there, even with the terror that darkened so many days. He shares with her his memories of what it was like to be the new immigrant, what it meant for him to make do, while he was broke and alone and yet always exhilarated by that ancient city.

He was so busy then, becoming fluent in Hebrew, getting himself educated, and embarking on a career that quickly turned into a secret other.

When he had his Hebrew to study, and his schoolwork to do, he would always take the bus up the mountain, even if his classes had been down on Givat Ram.

He'd hop off at the last stop and file past security, pausing for inspection by one of the old men (and they were always old), whose investigations consisted of pressing their fingers to the bottom of his book bag as if checking to see if it was ripe.

Z would settle into the library's fourth floor, feeling himself cocooned in a vision of Israel's brightest possible future. That's what he was trying to express to the waitress, how for him, for his dreams of what Israel might become, Mount Scopus summed it up.

Crammed together at those study tables were religious and secular, Arab and Jew, rich and poor, white and brown and (sometimes) black. The social groupings based on subject and course. The focus of the students—as with all universities the universe over—resting on the twin pillars of learning and getting laid.

That campus was a place of sex and study, a refuge from the attendant politics and attendant hatreds that constantly rattled the state. It was as if all of that noise was filtered out, and what was left was just pure hope. They were up on that mountain waiting for the inevitable harmony to set in, a promised change that had literally drawn Z from America. He had moved to Israel to contribute to that happy age. He had rushed his aliyah, transferring to Hebrew University in the middle of his graduate degree, because he was afraid if he stayed in America any longer, he'd miss it.

He was afraid peace would start without him.

Z admits, in response to the waitress's question, that of course there were the junior politicians in student government, and the junior idiots and crackpots on campus, who would one day, likewise, see their professional idiocies and crackpottitudes blossom. But the overarching, dominant goodness and happy idealism of the place easily drowned them out.

Nothing better demonstrated the unique normality of that oasis than the unstated policy that one could leave one's bag on a table and, for a few moments, walk away.

Really, outside of the university, Z could think of no other place in the whole country where a bag left unat-

tended wouldn't have the first person to spot it yelling out
without hesitation, the bomb squad summoned, a cordon
immediately thrown. So often and frequently did this happen that whenever anyone was late to a dinner or a drink, all
they would need say was, "Suspicious object"—everyone's
permanent, eternally reusable excuse. Z always remembers
the face of a businessman running back to fetch his forgotten briefcase just in time to see the sappers set it off, all his
papers swirling down onto the sidewalk after being blasted
into the air.

But on campus, no one expected you to drag all your
books from your favorite carrel to run out for a coffee or a
smoke or a quick pee.

When Z was hungry, which, in those days, in his slightly
younger man's body, he always ravenously was, he'd wend
through the absurdly byzantine main building and make
his way across the donor-named Nancy Reagan Plaza, to
the Frank Sinatra Cafeteria, which served—as far as he was
concerned—the best schnitzel in town.

Every school day for countless school days, he ate the
same thing: a colossal, state-subsidized plate of schnitzel,
rice, and gravy. A meal served to him by a kitchen staff that
was a mix of Israelis from West Jerusalem and Palestinians
from the neighboring village. Z felt warmly toward all of
them. It was the kind of fondness fostered by loyalty and
routine, and the nurturing inherent in being cared for.

Answering another question from the waitress, one
punctuated by a guffaw, Z admits that yes, he falls easily in
love with anyone who feeds him, and that when he finds a
lunch he likes, he does indeed eat it every day.

He also admits that he is telling the story this way because
he really wants her to grasp how important and special that

place was to him, and how singular its character, because he wants her to understand how perfectly-evilly-perfect it was to blow it up.

"Do you get it? They'd have to have known more than the layout of campus. They'd have to have truly understood its mentality to think they had a plan. This killer went into that always vibrant, truly mixed, and truly welcoming space and set his bag down among young people. He set his bomb down among all those bright futures and walked away. In this terrible time of suicide bombers, this wasn't a suicide. It was a bomb that needed goodwill to go off."

"And you knew it was Farid behind it?"

"Instantly. Even before credit was taken. Even before the final body count was released. I knew who did it, and why he did it, and what it was in response to—barely a week gone by. I also knew that the Mossad would be back up on Farid in a heartbeat, that they'd be on him ten times as hard, and that they'd be ten times more thorough. It wasn't the brother anymore. He wasn't the mark. Farid would now be the one."

"Isn't that good, in a way? Considering?"

"Not if you banked on him being different. Not if you maybe sent him significant state secrets, to try and change the outcome for both peoples. And even if you made your choices expressly to keep that cafeteria from blowing up. I mean, how long from that attack until they find the things I sent him? How long until they'd be up on me?"

"So what did you do?"

"I activated my mother."

"Your mother?"

"What else does a Jewish boy do when trouble is afoot?"

2014, Black Site (Negev Desert)

In his cell, curled fetal on the bed, Prisoner Z waits for the pill to kick in. He knows he'll have to weather the next horrific stretch of panic before he finds any relief. He looks up at the camera over the door, raising an arm to give the guard the finger and then offering it to the next camera and the next. When he is done, he returns to his previous entertainment and recommences the digging of nails into palms.

Prisoner Z closes his eyes, letting loose a cascade of anxiety-driven thoughts that he fears will finally break him. He attempts a positive visualization, willing the medicine to take effect.

He pictures his brain's receptors sifting through a river of molecules, plucking what they need from the stream rushing by. He struggles to make his whole self join in the effort.

Prisoner Z lying there, patient, patient, panning for gold.

The guard comes to visit when Prisoner Z is flat out, looking fully corpse-like. On the floor next to the bed, the guard sets two sweaty cans of Coke. Onto a prison tray, he dumps two servings of fries from their greasy sleeves.

"I brought ketchup too," he says.

He presents the squeeze bottle to his insensible prisoner, and then, turning it over, he squirts a bloody puddle.

Prisoner Z stares at the ceiling, unblinking, his arm hanging limp off the side of the mattress, knuckles dragging the floor.

"I drove all the way to the *steakiya*," the guard says. "With you knocked out, I wasn't afraid to leave the shop unmanned."

In response, no response. Prisoner Z does not stir.

"I know you're alive," the guard says. "It was clear from the monitors. Zombie-you looks different than dead you. Or, at least, I think it does, not yet having had the pleasure of seeing the real thing."

It is to this that Prisoner Z deigns to respond.

"You, sir, have drugged me good."

"I usually do give you point-two-fives. But I made a very sad face for the doctor, and he gave me the big-boy dose. That one was like a dozen of the usual." The guard considers Prisoner Z and, feeling benevolent, admits, "Watching the feed, I did kind of wonder if I'd lost you. But then you were doing that thing you always do with your mouth."

"I don't do anything with my mouth."

"Except that you do. Every time I dope you, you start with the dry mouth thing as soon as the pills start doing their job."

The guard feels quite proud for knowing. He wants to make clear that Prisoner Z is not the only one in town smart enough to read people. The guard can also observe and take note.

The guard dips a fry in the ketchup and dangles it over

Prisoner Z's face. Prisoner Z tips his head back and opens his mouth to receive it. Before the guard even moves, Prisoner Z opens his mouth for another.

The third fry Prisoner Z takes for himself, levering himself into a seated position.

"Was that so hard?" the guard says, fishing the backgammon board from his backpack. "Now why not drink your soda before it turns hot. We can play a couple of games. You can take advantage of your winning streak."

"It doesn't matter anymore, does it, if the game's never going to end?"

"You don't know it won't," the guard says, cheerful. "You can't tell what the future will bring. Maybe you'll be rescued tomorrow. Maybe the Palestinians will finally conquer us and make you ambassador to France. In the meantime, why not throw some dice and move a few checkers around?"

"I'll never forgive you," Prisoner Z says.

" 'Never' is a very long time."

"Did you even pass on my letters? All these years, and me pleading with a dead man. And you, letting me write him."

"I gave every one to my mother, as promised. Also, he wasn't dead. He wasn't even in a coma. They called it a semi-conscious state—it's different. They think he was listening. She read him every one."

"So that's you telling me you're a man of your word?"

"Aren't I? I mean, what's the difference? The General's response, healthy or sick, alive or dead—it's been kind of the same for you. He put you here to stay."

"It's kind of not the same. It's kind of earth-shatteringly different. You should have told me so I could have adjusted my strategy."

The guard shakes his head, it's so sad.

"What could you do from in here?"

"I'd have pressed you harder to make me exist again."

"You know I can't do that."

"And you know that's not true. You could make noise. If not from inside the system, you could have gone to the papers. You still can."

"If I do, they'll either censor the story or label me a conspiracy theorist, or a madman, or a drunk. They'll either humiliate me out there or toss me in here. We'd be roommates." Looking around at what is no better than a dungeon, the guard corrects himself. "Well, not in-here, in-here, but maybe in a real cell in a real prison. They'd give me a few years to ponder the bigness of my mouth."

"What's a few years to try and undo a life sentence that no one has had the dignity to hand down?"

"Okay," the guard says.

" 'Okay' what?"

"I'll think about it."

"You will?"

"Sure. And maybe you can advise me on the best way to go about it. I can't remember. How did taking an idiotic moral stand work out for you?"

2002, Paris

Z sits in his boss's office across from his boss's empty chair, while that same boss stands behind him, twisting a plastic rod and pivoting the slats to the venetian blinds closed in front of his glass wall, alerting everyone on the floor to yet another secret-business tête-à-tête.

If there were an action dumber, and more obvious, than the one Z's boss was engaged in, and in which he habitually engaged every time they needed to talk discreetly, Z would have liked to hear it.

The man he works for at the Parisian satellite of their global information technology concern is also his handler at his other job, with its alternate objectives and hole-and-corner realm. Together, they run this covert operation from inside the company, a situation facilitated by a sympathetic Zionistic soul among the higher-ups.

When his boss takes his seat, Z apologizes for the urgent nature of his request to meet, and the personal nature of the e-mail he sent the night before, but he wanted to loop his boss in just as soon as he himself was aware, and, well, it seems he is going to need an unscheduled leave.

Z wants to fly to the States to help his mother die or, you know, not die, he says. That is, he very much hopes she'll not die, but he also guesses she probably will.

"Riddled through," is the phrase Z lands on.

"I am so, so sorry," his boss says, with blunted affect.

"It's important to me—to her—that I be there."

"Of course."

"I should tell you, I went and bought a ticket, already, this morning."

"Yes," his boss says. "I know."

"You know?"

"We know. It came up. The ticket purchase."

"Yes," Z says. "I'd imagined it would," Z says, really not having imagined this at all.

The pretext itself—his mother's cancer, and his sudden need to race home to attend to her—he thought he'd set up expertly when he'd installed it as a contingency, years before. He had assumed, if he did ever need to employ it, that it wouldn't have been to extricate himself from a situation involving his genuinely well-meant treason.

On one of Z's early trips home to America to legally and preposterously change his name (an easy way to reboot an expat existence), he'd spent a jet-lagged morning in court waiting among a group of crazies who believed themselves to be a Petal or a Poppy, a Sunshine-Daydream or a Batman-James.

He'd driven back to his house, successful and fully exhausted, to find his dear mother waiting in the kitchen, wanting to know how his meeting had gone.

Her understanding was that he was visiting on business

(which, in some ways, he was), and, as relates to his made-up meeting, he'd said, thank you very much, it had gone just fine.

He removed his tie, and kissed her on the head, and went to the den. Once he was camped out on the sectional, the remote control in hand, he told her through the door-way, and as nonchalantly as he could, that—and it was very important to his work, she should know—he was entrust-ing her with a critical e-mail-related task.

So startling was this that his mother momentarily paused from offering him the fruit he never accepted and with which she continuously, unceasingly, plied him. She saun-tered into the space between her son and the TV, with a nice bowl of nectarines, and tried to sound nonchalant herself.

To be entrusted by her genius of a computer-expert son with any sort of responsibility like that was a highlight of her cyber-life.

"How can I help?" she'd said, as if it were no big deal at all.

Z praised her ability to check the weather on weather.com and to print out the digital pictures she received. He let her know he was full of confidence and told her that what he was asking was simple, besides. Simple, but still important.

He had a new e-mail account, he'd said, and he was list-ing her address as the default. She was never to write to him there. Never to tell anyone it even existed. But, if she ever did receive an alert about it, all she had to do was let him know.

It was an assignment that made her nervous just to hear.

"You can do it!" he'd said to his mother. "You're a pro."

He'd told her, almost as an afterthought, that she wasn't to waste time calling the number on which they shared their weekly catch-up, as there was a special, emergency number for such an occurrence. A number, like the e-mail address, that she was never, ever to use.

"Then how do I call you on it, if I'm never supposed to use it?"

"Except," he said, once again, "in this special case."

He did complicate it one step further. "I know this sounds kooky," he said. "But I'll also need you to make that call from somewhere else, when you do."

Not wanting to blow her chance at being a support, his mother had readily agreed.

And look at that? There he was, at news of the university bombing, stepping out of his office, returning to his apartment on Rue Domat, and knocking on a neighbor's door to tell them his Internet connection was down.

If he could, if it wouldn't be too much trouble, he'd said in his terrible French.

Then, in seconds, he'd logged on to that virgin account, changed his password, and logged back out. No e-mail sent, no contact made, an action as clean as clean could be.

He'd gone back to the apartment, and, from one of his hiding places, produced the never-used SIM that he always kept topped up with credit, and slipped it into the backup handset always kept charged to receive it.

He'd gone down into his building's lovely courtyard and waited for it to ring.

His mother, God bless her, it wasn't even thirty minutes before she was on the line, and—as he'd instructed— without calling his regular phone.

"Are you okay, honey?"

"I'm fine," he'd said.

"Someone changed your password. Do you know that?

They wrote me, the Internet people, to tell me that someone had changed a password."

"It's okay, Mom. I changed it."

"I almost didn't go on this morning—I do every morning, but today I have things to do. I was about to run out and now I'm so glad I checked. Should I forward the note to you?"

"No, Mother. Don't send it. And I'm so glad you checked too. And thanks for remembering to call this number first."

"I had it in my address book. I wrote it on the inside cover, 'Call special phone.' I tried the Erlbaums, but they weren't home, so I came to call from the JCC. They're letting me sit in the director's office. I said to bill me the long distance, but I bet they won't. They love me here."

"Perfect."

"And you're good? Is Paris hot? It gets so hot there in summer."

"It's cool today."

"Good. I worry about the heat. People die there in the summers."

"Old people, Mom."

"Like me!"

"Yes, their children are not good Jewish children. They all head off to their summer homes and leave the old grannies to cook."

"That's terrible."

"It is, Mother. And speaking of?"

"Speaking of cooking grannies?"

"Sort of, yes. I need you to call me on my regular number and tell me you're dying."

"What?" his mother said.

"I need you to make an appointment with your doctor

for today. You go in, you get him to send you for a scan. Then call me, even if it's the middle of my night. I need you to wake me and tell me you have cancer."

"Wait, do I have cancer? Do I? Oh my God! How do you even know?"

"I don't, Mother." Hearing the panic over the line, he'd repeated an emphatic, "You don't!"

"But how do you know I don't? Why even say it, if I'm not sick?"

"For personal reasons I need you to call me and tell me that you do. It needs to be bad. Tell me that the doctor wants to set you up at Sloan Kettering right away."

"What's happening?" she'd said, her voice shaky and filling Z with an excruciating surge of guilt. "What are you saying? Do I have cancer?"

"Mother, no. You don't. But I need you to call and tell me you do."

His mother went quiet for some time, and then she'd started to weep.

"Don't cry, Mother. You're fine."

"It's not me," she'd said. "It's you. It's happened. You've gone psychotic. I always sensed."

"I'm fine, Mom. We're both fine."

"Oh, you're a bit too old. Trust me, I waited. I thought we were safe by now. But you've always shown signs. Oh my, oh my."

"I'm not psychotic."

"Your grandfather was psychotic."

"Wait, what?" Z said, drawn off on a tangent he didn't expect. Secrets everywhere, he thought. Secrets abound.

"We never told you."

"Which grandpa? Is it Grandpa Mike?"

"Your father's father. Zayde Reuben."

"How could you not tell me that before?"

"Because we wanted to avoid this. Your father and I, we thought if we didn't say, then maybe."

"Knowing medical history doesn't give you psychosis. Anyway, I'm pretty sure that sort of thing skips a generation."

She hesitated on her end, and then she said, "Skipped a generation, that's you."

Z thought about it. Yes, on that point, she was right.

"Well, I'm not psychotic. But I still need you to do this. I can explain when I'm home."

"Home Israel? Or home, here? If you're sick you can come back to your room, it's just the same as ever. We pray every night for you to get out of that godforsaken country."

"France?"

"Israel."

"You sent money to Israel your whole life. You march in the stupid parade. You love Israel."

"I do. But not for my son. And France is even worse. Tell me what's going on! Who are you in trouble with? Tell me, and I'll do like you say."

"I really can't. And don't try and guess. But I need you to get an appointment and then a mammogram and then call. And make sure it goes through insurance right away too."

"I hate that machine, squishing down."

"I'm sorry, Mother. But you should get one every year. How long has it been?"

She didn't answer.

"I'd come up with something else, a better idea, if I thought it was for nothing. A woman your age should get checked."

"What if they find it?"

"Then maybe they can save you, and then you'll sound more realistic on the phone."

"You're a terrible son."

"I know. But if you do it, I really can come home. I can get a place near you and Dad, forever. No more travel, I promise."

"If I tell you the cancer thing?"

"Yes, if you do that all today. If you get in somewhere and call me, and never tell anyone about the talk we're having now. Just delete the alert, and do like I say. I'll call and check in on you a bunch of times, okay? Just be yourself. Be your paranoid, negative, hopeless self. Only, add the cancer."

"Because you're in trouble?"

"Because your son is in some trouble. Yes."

It's this notion of trouble that Z is very much distracted by as his boss says, "I hope you don't think it crass of us." And his boss, reading that distraction expertly well, says, "Us, taking advantage of your mother's illness in this way."

"Of course not," Z says.

"We must harness what we can, even when it means playing on the emotions of others. It's the unfortunate nature of our work."

"I don't understand?" Z says, in what might as well be his patented catchphrase.

"We thought, this trip of yours, charged as it is, is also a perfect way to get you to Tel Aviv under the radar."

"Instead of America?"

"On the way to America. They just want a day of your time, to debrief you about Berlin. We were already talking about how to get you back for a visit without drawing attention, and then this very unfortunate alibi came up, and we thought, yes, why not?"

"You want me to change my flights? So they can talk to me in Israel?"

"To debrief you about Berlin, yes. But also, no," his boss says. "We don't need you to change your flights. We've already taken the liberty." Here his boss reaches into a desk drawer and presents an itinerary and set of tickets to Z.

Z reads the schedule, trying to seem absolutely, beyond at ease with the change.

His boss leans across the desk and points at the paper.

"That lists it as direct to New York. But the tickets are obviously correct. The Tel Aviv leg is there."

It's so smart, and so simple, Z thinks. He is found out already, and they are asking him to transport himself home for retribution. No muss, no fuss. Easy as pie.

Z looks to his boss with what must be obvious terror on his face. Revealing, he knows. Still, what can Z do in the moment but forge ahead?

"It's a perfect idea," Z says. "A great way to pop me in and out unnoticed. But the reason I asked to talk, and forgive me for the confusion, was the opposite."

"Of what?"

"Of what you're proposing," Z says. "I wanted you to know that after I e-mailed you, and after I booked the ticket that I, of course, knew you'd see—my mother called again. We had a good long talk. And things are different."

"She doesn't have cancer?"

"No, she still does. Bad cancer. It's that, with the chemo, and the radiation, the rounds and rounds—it will go on for some time. And she knows how much pressure I'm under at work. That is, at the work she knows as my work."

"Okay," his boss says.

"So, it's already urgent, but what she was saying is that it would stay urgent and that I should save up my leave. That it would be better if I came for the Jewish holidays. She is brave, my mother. She said, typical her, that it would give her time to get used to being a sick person. She said, having her son there for Rosh Hashanah, it's only a few weeks away, and it would give her something to live for."

His boss swivels in his chair, considering. His face shows nothing, a picture of restraint.

"I appreciate your point," his boss says. "Regardless, why not start an unofficial leave now? Stay close, recharge your batteries, and let me talk to Tel Aviv."

2002, Paris

They sit on the couch in their suite in what is turning into their go-to position, the waitress leaning against its arm on a heap of pillows, her feet in Z's lap. Z squeezes a foot and lifts it, admiring her ancient pedicure, the paint mostly missing, the polish picked off. He kisses those toes, and he loves those toes.

"Do you know where you messed up, Jewish boy?" the waitress asks.

"No," is Z's answer. He cannot fathom where, along his pitiable route, that might be.

"It's believing a Jewish mother would be able to get you out of a problem this big. If you need the world to spin in the other direction, get an Italian girl to ask her father. That's when you'll see what an overprotective Calabrese can do."

"Ha!" Z says. "You're serious?"

"I am. You should meet my dad. He could help."

"Because he's rich?"

"No, not because he's rich. Because of *how* he's rich. He owns a small media empire—which is still quite large."

Z rubs a foot. He offers nothing in response beyond "So?"

"You really don't know anything about our country, do you?"

Z, apparently, does not.

"In Italy, if it's 'media,' Berlusconi owns a piece. My father has the prime minister's ear, and a good amount of his money."

"That's the plan? Your father?"

The waitress takes her foot back and sits up at Z's side.

"Do you have one better than living in this hotel forever?"

"There are worse ideas," Z says, of their palatial digs.

"If you have one better, let's hear it. Anyway, I still don't understand why you don't take a taxi to the airport and just go."

Z smiles at her sweetly and pats her leg.

"I'm starting to hope they catch you," the waitress says.

"Sorry," he says, sincerely not intending to condescend. "I don't run, because I don't have diplomatic cover. I'm just someone with a bad passport, who has broken a lot of laws. If Israel tips off France and then denies knowing me, I rot in jail here. If they have me flagged and take ownership, I get deported and sit in prison there. In both cases, I lose. Only, Israel also loses, because I come with a sizable international incident attached. And so we're in a standoff. Which leaves me stuck here, trying not to give my colleagues the chance to have me slip in the shower or break my neck on the stairs. My only out is to get to America, where, for a bucket of reasons, it becomes worth it for all of us to just walk away. Maybe I look over my shoulder a bit more, but at least at home I fit in and the Israelis stand out. If we're playing the odds, I still likely win."

"But you can't get there."

Z practically hoots at the sad truth of it.

"No, I can't."

"Then it sounds like your best bet is to come to Italy with me. You can throw yourself on my father's mercy—something he very much enjoys."

"Since when are you going to Italy?" Z says, caught off guard yet again, which, occupationally, really shouldn't happen to him so much.

"Since always. It's high season on Capri. We never miss it, my family," the waitress says. "It's not the trip that's sudden, it's your knowing that is."

She stands now and, looking toward the staircase to the bedroom, extends a hand, which he takes.

"Were you just going to leave me?"

"Wouldn't you?"

No, is what Z thinks, getting up. He really wouldn't leave her.

As for the great throng of people lining up to rescue him, the waitress is offering the only option he has. Access to someone with access, it could help.

"What if we get there and your father doesn't want to get involved? What if he turns me in?"

"To who? The hotel bartender? This is what excites him in a life where little does. He'll be thrilled. In any event, you haven't broken any laws in Italy, which makes you better off there than here. And if they catch you on the island a week from now, instead of here tomorrow? At least we can fuck the whole time while we stay in the finest hotel I've ever seen."

Z chews at his lip.

"Better than this?"

"By far! There's more to look at out the window than

some old obelisk. Have you ever seen the Faraglioni up close?"

"No," Z says, he hasn't. "Your plan, it actually kind of does make sense."

"Because of the fucking?"

"Yes," he says. "Because of that. Only, how am I supposed to get there? The passport issue is the same."

"You really are the worst. They must have trained you at some point."

"Logistics was not my strong suit. I was best at knowing when I was being followed. Paranoia is where I shined."

"Well, we can drive all the way," she says. "Right up to the ferry. There's no reason to stop us in a car, if you can manage not to look as terrified as you do right now. Paris to Naples. EU country to EU country, with a little luck we won't even have to slow down at the border to wave. I bet we can do it in twelve hours, not much more."

"Like New York to Chicago?"

"If you say so. Either way, *chi non fa non sbaglia.*"

"What does that mean?"

"If you don't try, you don't fail."

"That's not exactly calming considering the consequences. Do you have something better?"

"*Vedi Napoli e poi muori,*" she says. "See Naples and then die."

2002, Paris

"You said you'd come home! You said you'd be by my side."

"Please, Mother, please."

"I'm dying, and you're not here."

"Complications, Mother. I'm on my way."

"You keep saying that, but you don't show, and the days tick by. The doctors. The prognosis. I won't be here long. And you, waking a sick woman in the middle of the night."

Z waits and he waits, and he really can't tell, is no longer sure.

"Are you really dying, Mother? Was the news really that bad?"

"Who lies about such a thing? What kind of monster?" Here she begins weeping. "I tell my own son I'm dying, and still he doesn't come."

"I'm on my way, Mother. You can't imagine what's gone wrong."

"So tell me."

Z doesn't tell her. He doesn't say a word. Not about the

hotel room in which he stands, or the car parked outside, or the woman he is smitten with, who waits impatiently at the door.

He offers the waitress a hangdog grimace and holds up a finger, he needs just a minute more, pacing with the hotel phone.

Let his pursuers track it. Let them see where he's calling from. When they arrive, he'll already be gone.

"Hello? Are you still there?" his mother says.

"I am, Mother. And I'm doing everything I can to get home. You cannot know."

"What I know is that my only child isn't here. And at a time like this! I told your father, we should have had a second. Back in the seventies, what family only had one? I told him, I told him when I was nice and fertile. What if the first is a rotten egg?"

"Please calm down, Mother, I'm doing my best."

"Your best will have you showing up to put me in the ground. Your best will get you a welcoming kiss from your mother after her lips have turned blue."

"What are you saying? Are you really sick?"

"Of course I am. I have cancer. I am dying, dying, dying. And you with your secrets. What kind of child have I raised?"

Z starts to answer.

"Don't," she says. "Spare me. I already know. It's just as I told your father. We've got ourselves a rotten egg."

The waitress drives, with Z in the passenger seat sporting dark sunglasses (one of the few props he'd stuffed in his bag). Z keeps an eye on the side mirror and attempts his best impression of someone relaxed, well aware that he appears rigid, and miserable, and like he's up to no good. He can't shake the dispiriting exchange with his dying or not-dying mother.

It's she who always used to warn him, "Never steal anything. And, if you do, never get caught. You look like a murderer when you feel guilty. Even innocent, they'd hang you for that face."

He goes to share the memory with the waitress, but somehow it shames him, and he tells the waitress this instead: "When we were learning countersurveillance, we had this really brilliant instructor who was—no matter how well we did—disappointed in us. She'd always say, 'The biggest challenge at a Jewish spy service is training everyone not to look so guilty. A less nervous nation might, as the anti-Semites believe, truly take over the world.' "

They cruise along the highway, making progress, unimpeded. It's beautiful, windows-rolled-down weather and once they've put a couple of hours between themselves and Paris, once Z manages to stop jumping at every siren and horn honk, to stop stiffening at the sight of every car switching into their lane, he begins, at least outwardly, to resemble a person calming down.

They listen to the radio and sing to the eighties American classics and the *"Ella, elle l'a"* France Gall–style French hits in perpetual play.

In those first four hours they stop to get waters and chocolate, to pee and gas up, and to buy a pack of cigarettes to smoke out of boredom along the way. As the kilometers roll by, and the road rolls on, and the day unfolds, they make good time.

When they near the border, Z feels the muscles in his

neck seize up, his whole body gone tight. The waitress reaches over and pats a knee. She coos at him, as one might at a child or a dog. Z takes a breath and holds it.

Together, they drive into Italy as if there's no border at all, passports in their pockets, her foot on the gas.

2014, Jerusalem

Ruthi has her lazy son drag up a rusted bathtub from among the weeds in the empty lot below. She makes him punch holes in the bottom for extra drainage and paint the outside a nice no-evil-eye blue. There is a perfect spot for it on the balcony, right by the door, that gets excellent light but nothing too harsh.

She sends the guard to the garden shop to buy dirt and fertilizer and mulch. When the tub is loaded up, and a healthy bed made, she sends him back for young tomato plants and tells him to let the nice Iraqi boy who works there choose.

Ruthi sinks a stake at each end of the tub and runs string in between for a trellis. She plants her seedlings, tamping the dirt down: she waters them and then spends the day in her housecoat watching them grow. By nightfall, she is sure they're already taller. The Jerusalem air, it is miraculously healthy for all God's creations.

The guard notes that the window boxes hanging from the balcony's rails have been pruned to perfection. The outdoor tiles gleam, and lining the wall of the house on the other side of the door from that tub is a row of tin cans pot-

ted with herbs that have hardly broken the soil. Alongside
them, a trio of avocado pits, impaled on toothpicks and half
submerged, wait to sprout their wild roots in glass jars.

When the guard is ready for bed, he goes out to smoke
and finds his mother, still in her housecoat, standing in the
moonlight and staring at that bathtub. She holds, in her
hand, a glass of wine.

The guard comes up behind her and, leaning down, rests
his chin on her shoulder.

"You know," he says, "we live right by the market. You
can buy tomatoes for a penny each. It's stupid to grow them
here."

"They taste better when they're yours."

"Also, when you make a blessing before eating them,
they're ten times as sweet."

"You mock," she says, "but that's true too."

"Don't become a crazy woman, Ruthi, that's all I'm asking." He calls her by her first name, as he does whenever
he's being fresh.

The guard straightens up and lights his joint.

"And don't wait around for another prime minister to
end up in a coma. That job is a hard one to get twice."

"What should I do then to keep busy?"

"Volunteer. Go back to school. Start a new career. Challenge yourself, *Ima.* Keeping watch on tomatoes is not so
hard."

"Who would hire me at this point, at this age? What am I
good at but caring for dying men who take forever to let go?"

"You and me, both," he says. "The family business."

She studies him and sips her wine, her grown-up son,
who never bloomed. Maybe the air here didn't do everything she thought.

Ruthi reaches up and pinches his cheek, hard enough that he pulls her hand away.

"And you? Don't you hang your whole life on one person. Hero or villain, when they're gone, you are left without any personal meaning of your own."

"Don't say that, *Ima*. Not about yourself. You were hired by the General, but you were working always for Jerusalem. Why not go back down into it? Walk around. See how the city you've slaved for has changed."

Wise boy, she thinks. Wise boy. Maybe he has matured more than she knows.

2002, Capri

They sleep in the car near Molo Beverello and wake to get the early ferry from port. As soon as that hydrofoil lifts itself above the water, Z dares to unbend. He is thrilled to watch Naples turn small behind them.

When they disembark at Capri, Z and the waitress take a canopied taxi up the winding drive to the top of the island and the edge of the main square.

The waitress leads Z through it, and then down the charming laneways, where she stops at all the boutique windows— they'll both need to come back for proper clothes.

They take a cliff-top path that dead-ends at the hotel's overlook. It's just as she'd promised, hanging above the Faraglioni and the wide-open sea.

It has been some time since Z has been breathless from anything but fear.

"You grew up doing this?" he says to her.

"I grew up doing this, yes. The Crillon in Paris. The Punta Tragara in Capri. In every place there is one hotel, considered to be 'the hotel,' and that is where we stay."

"But you still felt the need to do the fake-modest, honest-work, too-many-roommates thing."

"It's a rite of passage wealthy parents insist upon so their children don't become beasts. Or, at least, so we learn how to pretend we are thankful."

Z walks to the guardrail at the edge of the piazza. The waitress tells him to stay put and commune with nature while she checks them in.

He takes in the majesty in every direction, settling his gaze on the bay below, and all those humongous yachts—ten times bigger than the ones in Berlin. He finds that he misses sailing with Farid. This confuses, for Farid is, however distant from the acts, a killer. And further confusing is accepting that, however distant from that one-ton bomb, Z is a killer himself.

Z is pulled from this wretched reverie by a loving yank. The waitress, hooking a finger through one of his belt loops, draws him close.

She's returned with a room key on a giant brass knob. This she hangs off the first finger of her non-jeans-tugging hand.

He puts an arm around her—feeling cared for—and pulls the waitress back his way. It feels so sweetly couple-like. It feels, to Z, what life could be on the other side of this hellacious ordeal.

"Let's go get you some burrata," she says, "and a bowl of vodka. We'll fuck and take a nap, and then I'm going to stick you on this metal ledge in one of the pools. It has a million tiny holes in it, and each one of those holes is a tiny jet. You can lie there like a sausage cooking red under the sun, while all those little bubbles take your worries away."

"Shouldn't we say hi to your parents first? Or, at least, tell them you've brought along a spy on the run? It's a pretty big surprise."

"You really don't understand the rich, do you?"

Z, evidently, does not. No more than he understood Italy and its media moguls, before.

"If you have all the money in the world, it's boring just to get more money. The only things left that hold any interest are sex and power."

"And how does that break down in my case?"

"For me, sex. For my father, a wonderful, international game of power."

The hotel room is a chichi duplex, with an open staircase to a lofted bedroom and, off the living room, a wraparound balcony hanging out into infinity. Z did not think it possible, but it's even fancier than their Parisian suite.

If one didn't know that everything was coming down around him, one would reckon, from his lakeside mansion in Berlin all the way to this extravagant space with this extraordinary woman, that Z must be doing something right.

They eat and drink, they have sex and take a nap, repeating the cycle throughout the day until they finally spread out naked on the lounge chairs on their balcony to watch the sun set.

When the room phone rings, the waitress takes her time getting it. When she says, *"Pronto,"* into the receiver, Z thinks he may die of love.

She listens, and covers the mouthpiece, and whispers too loudly, "Get in the shower. Clean up as best you can." When she hangs up she says, "We really should have run back down to the shops for some decent clothes."

They wait at a candlelit table down the stairs from the lower pool. They are perched on the edge of a private strip of hotel terrace, overlooking the black water and the endless, immeasurable world.

The waitress's father, who is strapping and gray-templed and younger and stronger than Z might have imagined, takes a moment to shake Z's hand, before disappearing back into an extended round of hugging and laughing and talking to his daughter in Italian at great speed. Z cannot imagine how young her mother must be, as her father looks like he had her when he was ten years old.

At some point, which Z thinks is a long time after his arrival, the waitress says to her father, in English, "We're being rude."

Taking their seats, she says to Z, "Typical mother," and shakes her head. And her father, in silver suit to match his hair, and white shirt open a button too far, says, "My wife will join us in a couple of days. Evidently, there's still something left in Milan that she hasn't yet bought."

"She's selfish," the waitress adds, as explanation.

"Now, *Porcospino*, that's not nice," her father says.

Then he slaps Z on the back, with some force. "Do you know why she's upset, your girlfriend?"

"No, sir," Z says, feeling like he's ten years old himself.

"Your girlfriend is upset because, without her mother here to keep me distracted, you two are stuck with me. We are all on a lavish three-person date."

"It's a nightmare!" the waitress says, sounding serious, while her father beams at her with a proud smile.

It's not until all the dinner plates have returned to the

kitchen that the waitress, in a very politic manner, utters the truth about Z.

Her father, studying his guest like a pinned butterfly, says, quite loudly, "A spy?"

"He is," the waitress says.

As the desserts are marched out and placed on the table, the waitress's father takes hold of the server's arm.

To Z, he says, "This calls for some whiskeys." And from the waiter he's restrained, her father orders a round.

While they poke at their sweets, a global version of Z's problems is shared.

The waitress's father nods knowingly, turning to his daughter to assess her, and then to Z to do the same. "That's quite a story," he says, markedly unruffled.

"You're taking it well," Z says. "Me being in trouble, and all. And needing such serious help. It's really kind."

"Believe it or not," her father says, clamping a hand down on Z's wrist, "this girl, she is a monster," and here he releases Z to press the back of that hand, most delicately, against his daughter's cheek. "She's nicer than her mother. But, still, a terrible headache. These? Your problems? They are not so bad. You are—even as a fugitive spy—not yet close to the worst boyfriend she's ever had."

2002, Tyrrhenian Sea

At breakfast, the waitress's father says, "One seat on a private flight, where they don't so much as peek at who is aboard. Is that all you're after?"

Z offers a diffident nod.

"And you have a passport?"

"A couple," he says, with a sad laugh. "But, yes, I have one with me."

"So this is your big disaster? You need someone with blurry eyesight to put a stamp on a page, or maybe have Customs check the cabin while you're locked in the bathroom taking a piss?"

"Yes, sir," Z says. "That would be a dream."

"I thought this was a big favor? You didn't need to come to me for this, you could merely have come to Naples. Do you know how many metric tons of contraband have already, this morning, moved through? One nice Jewish boy would easily disappear into the mix."

"Should I take the ferry back? If there's someone who can really make that happen—"

"Tomorrow, maybe," her father says, patting Z on the

hand. "I have a couple of calls out. But you, my son, are in Italy on a Sunday. You should have chosen a country less Catholic if you wanted to accomplish something today. Also, if you're expecting my help you should keep your own commitment. I've rented us a beautiful yacht for a sail, and you two promised to be my date."

Z feels himself turning pale.

"What?" her father says, missing nothing.

The waitress, who is busy rubbing her father's sunscreen into her arms, pipes in, "He's a terrible sailor. And part of it is why he's in the mess he's in. I think it's trauma."

Her father picks up his sunglasses from the table and puts them on, apparently so he can immediately remove them to strengthen his look of surprise.

"I'm not asking him to captain, *Porcospino*. I'm asking him not to fall off the side." To Z, he says, "There'll be excellent food and excellent service. And I've made a reservation at my favorite restaurant in the world for tonight. The only way to get there is by the water."

He then takes out his wallet and hands a credit card to Z.

"Why don't you both run down and get some bathing suits and whatever else you need. My daughter says you're traveling a bit light."

Z takes the credit card and stares at it. He tries to smile, and it comes out a sort of pained smirk.

"What?" her father says. "I took it for granted that you were a natural at signing other people's names. Please," he says, leaning in, "do it for me. Let's put the intrigue aside and have a lovely day."

"It's just the calls," Z says, trying not to plead. "If something comes through. Shouldn't we stay here where we can better be reached?"

The waitress's father reaches down and pulls a coral-colored sweater off a daypack sitting by his feet. With no shortage of fanfare, he fishes out a very impressive-looking satellite phone. "If we lose cell service, Sputnik will find us. I never ski without a beacon, and I never sail without one of these. You, James Bond, might as well relax."

"He hates those kinds of jokes," says the waitress, rubbing lotion into the tops of her ears.

"So you told me. But I don't care. It's a father's prerogative. I get to torture any boy you bring home."

They sail the day away on a massive schooner. They eat and drink at a long wooden table. It's truly a decadent lunch. They swim off an island Rudolf Nureyev used to own, and the waitress's father, looking drunk, yells orders up at the crew from the water with a sort of happy gusto. For Z, he sometimes switches to English, as he does when they set sail again, to say things like, "I've told them to show us what this boat can really do."

The crew listens, for they pick up quite a bit of speed, and quite a bit of wind, and the waitress drags Z away from her father and over to a mattress on the bow, where she hugs him, under a blanket, while the boat bucks.

Z's bare feet turn cold, sticking out from under, while the rest of him feels snug, curled against the waitress, his face buried in her hair.

As if following the pace of the day, they slow as the sun dips, changing course—the waitress's father explains—for the restaurant. "You'll go wild for it," he says, standing over them, with yet another whiskey in his hand. "It's a private cove, with a private beach. It's the only thing there."

"It's too shallow for a boat like this," the waitress says. "We moor ourselves, and they send out a skiff to fetch us."

"Before you even have your napkins in your lap, they bring out plates of sea urchins, still squirming from the lemon juice in their shells."

"It's Prince Charles's favorite," the waitress says.

"It is," her father confirms. "But who knows if he has any taste at all."

It's good to be rich, is what Z thinks. And good to be powerful. And, without liking her father even a whit more, he is beginning to think that a man this confident and horrible can indeed get him that one seat on that one private plane, where scrutiny will come second to comfort.

This is what he is mulling, when he breaks free of the waitress's loving arms and heads over to the port side, to try to spot the restaurant.

Z can already hear the engine of the boat coming for them. He can see its light shining, and beyond it, only darkness. The restaurant and its cove seem very far away.

Her father sidles up, and Z says, "It looks like a long ride to dinner. I can't see the shore from here."

"That's why it's a cove," her father says. "It's tucked into the coast. You'll see it when we get around the bend. Also, sailor, you must know it's not easy to see straight across water. If you want to see far, look up. The moon, I promise, is distant from here." As he says this, his face is lit by the light of the approaching craft, and Z sees that he holds the satphone in his hand. "Go get your girlfriend," he says. "Our lift is here."

One of the crew turns up with a huge flashlight, which he aims out into the night. Z can see the black tubes of the gunwale gliding their way.

A line is thrown, and the ladder is lowered.

As ordered, Z goes over to the waitress, who is wearing

jeans over her bathing suit and, in her bikini top, has that blanket wrapped around her shoulders against the chill.

They stand together, his arm slipped under the blanket and pressed to her bare back, as they watch her father reach down a hand to help pull up the man sent to shuttle them.

It is strange, Z observes, for this man to board when they should be climbing down to join him. It is stranger still how much that very large man, in his windbreaker, looks like the waiter from the restaurant in Paris. As if every burly employee in the service industry had one single face.

As Z makes terrible sense of what he's seeing, he feels he wants to say something to the waitress, who stands beside him, the blanket already dropped to the deck.

Before he speaks, he sees that she is holding a wet-looking burlap sack, itchy and worn. He wonders where she suddenly got it from and imagines it might have been right there the whole trip, tucked under a coil of rope.

He looks toward the giant Huguenot, who is speaking to the waitress's father in Hebrew and gripping a fistful of zip ties.

"You see?" Z says to the waitress, and now Z is speaking in Hebrew too, for he knows his beloved must speak particularly well. "I told you. I'm a professional. I spotted that one right off. Even with your father—I thought, he looks too young, and the way he stares at you. This guy, something is off. I don't miss a thing."

"But you missed me," the waitress says.

"Maybe I wanted to miss you."

"That's sweet. Very romantic. But still, a *fashla* of *fashlot*. In the end, you fucked up good."

"Don't I get any credit for picking this one out in Paris?" he says, pointing with his chin.

"Don't you think you were maybe supposed to?"

The waitress gives Z time to consider. The Huguenot, looking over, points to his watch, and the man who is not her father says, "*Nu,* Shira!" hurrying the waitress along.

Shira nods and points Z to a chair that, like a magic trick, has suddenly appeared. He sits atop it, wondering what would happen if he dared move, how far he would get. He tries to picture what it would look like to flip that chair and dive over the side with a splash.

"Even if I give you Paris," the waitress says, "even if making the waiter that first time was a good catch. What about missing everything else that got you to here?"

"Unfortunately, with espionage, there's a lot of gut feel to it," he says. "It is, of all things, an inexact science."

The waitress seems to accept that, and Z, though he'd like to talk more about it, says, "And the restaurant on the beach?"

"Oh, it's there. It's honestly excellent. A gem."

"And Prince Charles?"

"He really favors it. It's true."

Z looks at the men, who are looking at him, and he looks to the waitress, who has slipped behind him, and then out at the water behind her. "The Mediterranean," he says, "it's beautiful even like this."

"This part," she says, "is called the Tyrrhenian Sea."

Z takes a long, deep breath of that open-water air and turns to face forward. He looks up at the useless sliver of moon lighting nothing, and out into the night, which one would generally call pitch-black. But, of course, that kind of gloom is nothing. Nothing compared to what it's like as his beloved lowers that sack, nothing like the darkness as the hood comes down.

2014, Gaza Border (Israeli side)

In the mornings Shira walks the kibbutz. Out past the cafeteria and the infirmary and the laundry, to the greenhouses
where the Thai workers toil. She strolls by a graveyard for
giant tires and old tractor parts and hurries past the plastics
factory spitting out the packing foam and bubble wrap that
keep this farming collective afloat.

Circling back toward her rented cottage, she admires
a sturdy desert rosebush climbing the side of a sun-dulled
house. Across from it is the kindergarten, and Shira lin-
gers outside, enamored by the perfect incompatible-
compatibility of the place. It's a reinforced, bunker-like,
cement building, ready to take a direct hit. Its doors are
wide open, and inside a pair of teachers lead the little ones
through a song.

Many of the families with relatives up north have gone
north. She knows that these children who remain belong to
the stalwarts and stubborn, to those whose jobs—skilled
and unskilled—demand that they stay, and also to those
with no other options from which to choose.

Shira also knows that one or two or three of these beau-

tiful moppets belong to parents who are simply and amaz-
ingly unaware. Parents who suffer from an advanced sort
of Israeliness. No matter the seriousness of a threat, they
are constitutionally incapable of processing menace. Their
lives, every day, continue as if nothing out of the ordinary is
going on.

Her thought is interrupted by the ring of a bicycle's bell.
Shira is blocking the path.

She steps aside, and no sooner has the young woman
riding gone past than she brakes and hops from her seat. A
trailer, with what looks like hot pepper plants, is hitched to
the bicycle's frame.

Shira already knows what's coming. It is the thanks she
will be offered for coming down to stay, when so many from
there had understandably left.

"We appreciate your coming to support us," the woman
says.

Then she rolls a pedal to the top of its arc, ready to
push on.

"How about you? You're still here." Shira speaks with a
kind of urgency, trying to trap this woman in conversation.
She can hear a tone of great loneliness in her own voice.

"This is my home. I can't very well be showing support
for myself."

"Still, it seems brave to me, your cruising around with
those peppers—are they peppers?—with all this going on."
Shira makes a motion meant to include the missiles whistling, and the Israeli boys who are missing, and the war that
is brewing, the tanks parked in the fields along the border.
But, as she signals the overall atmosphere with a wave of her
hand, embraced in it are the children at play, and the house
with the roses, and this striking and welcoming girl on a
bicycle conversing with her in the dry morning breeze.

The girl is all warmth, and infers what she likes, and answers the more direct of the questions posed. "Chilcostles," she says, of her chilies. "They're not native to here, but they grow very well."

The girl pulls at the arms of her T-shirt, making more room for her muscles. She dials the pedal back around, a full rotation, preparing her getaway once more.

She is, Shira thinks, in a great rush to raise those peppers up.

"It doesn't scare you, what's coming?" Shira says. "Not an invasion? Not the rockets that already fall?"

"What's to be scared of? It's a gorgeous day. We have the best army in the world, right here to protect us. And there is also God's will."

"It's a lot to ask of the army . . . and of God. You could ask a lot less from farther away."

"If this kibbutz wasn't here, there'd be another barrier, closer in, and someone else's home would be on the line. It's a duty and a privilege to live here—"

"At the front?" Shira says.

"In paradise."

The girl then heaves her weight down on the pedal and rides off.

Shira watches her go and knows she'd forgotten to add this type of person to her list. The vibrant young altruist happily putting her body in harm's way.

She thinks about this as she walks in the direction the girl and her bicycle have gone. The path leads her out to the western edge of the kibbutz, and Shira follows it right up to the security fence. She stares through to its twin, across a dirt track, and beyond that into Gaza.

Between those fences—between her and her mapmaker—an Israeli army jeep rumbles along, driving the perimeter road. Caged in as they are, the soldiers look to Shira more like prisoners than border patrol.

The boys in the back wave as they tick by, or more, Shira thinks, they lift up, in a friendly manner, the guns in their grips. Shira waves in return, wishing she could tell them what a fine job they're doing. She wishes too that she could whisper a secret in their ears. She wants to tell them they're missing the point.

They tool around, tough, vigilant, keeping careful eye on both sides of their dusty route.

And underneath them, Shira knows, run the tunnels.

2002, Black Site (Negev Desert)

It was after his capture, and transport. After being shipped across the Mediterranean, like the human cargo that he was. After days chained standing until he'd have given his life just to sit, and then days forced into seated positions that made him yearn for the chains. After being interrogated until he took credit for what he'd done, and further interrogated until he took credit for things of which he'd never dreamed, Prisoner Z was allowed to sleep for a stretch. Then he was moved once more.

It was quiet in that new cell. He'd sat there, hands tied behind his back, suffocating blind in his sack. He'd tried to control his breathing, deafening as it had become. He'd struggled to pick up any ambient sound.

Time went by. Great swaths of it, he was fairly sure. He'd decided that, whatever came next, he must have, at least, reached some sort of end. This is when he'd meet his lawyer. This is when he'd get to call his worrying mom. He'd face his public shame. Then the clock would start on the gigantical debt to society that they'd deem he owed.

When nothing changed. When he thought he might die

of thirst, or starve to death. When he thought, maybe it was not a cell he was in, and that—an alternate, cruel judgment already passed—he'd been buried alive, that's when he heard a door open. That's when the guard first came in.

This memory, Prisoner Z accepts, may be fully colored by his disordered retrospect, but he believes deeply that he immediately knew. Just from the sound of those heavy shoes on the floor, from the way that cell gave off its first echo, from the pace of the man, and the lag between entrance and action. There was something about it that already contained all the hopelessness of Prisoner Z's plight.

He had understood that what he'd imagined as some sort of finish was only the beginning, the unfading start.

He could feel the guard standing there. He could feel it exactly as if the guard were standing over him right now. There was no talking. No touching. Not even a good, loving kick to the ribs.

Then, like that, came a sudden, simple shift in realities. The falconer reaching down and pulling the hood from his hawk's head.

Prisoner Z cannot shake that agonizing image. That first moment in the cell when he shifted from one darkness to the next.

2014, Gaza Border (Israeli side)

Oh, how she misses him on the other side of that fence. Somewhere there, trapped among the two million, is her mapmaker, the unanticipated love of her life. If Shira knew when she first saw him what that waiting would be like, she'd not have let herself dream of seeing him again.

Then she laughs. Fuck that first sighting, Shira thinks, remembering instead their first fucking. And she knows that it's not true.

She still can't believe it. Adventure had always been her thing, but spontaneity, that was a different animal. Yet there she'd found herself, wooed and wooing, wrestling with her sexy adversary in a hotel bed.

They'd taken a shower after and ended up having sex again, steaming up the bathroom until they thought the wallpaper might come loose. She'd sent him back to the bedroom and came out to meet him, a towel wrapped around her hair. Her mapmaker was atop the sheets, grinning ear to ear.

"This is why those who don't want peace don't want

it," he'd said, in his perfect Hebrew. "The minute we get to know each other—"

He didn't get to finish as Shira lay down on top of him and bit the end of his nose.

"Yes," she said. "Let us loose and the mutually assured ravishing begins."

She tossed the towel to the floor and rested her head on his chest, her wet curls cold, she could tell, from his shiver. He closed his arms around her, and together they stared up at the complicated glass fixture on their ceiling, fit for a museum. He had not skimped on their rendezvous room.

Cuddled up like that, the mapmaker stated, with a getting-to-know-you tone, "I'm assuming," he said, "that you are a spy."

She reached up to grab, and then hit him with, a pillow.

"You waited until after the sex to say that?"

"Just because I believe in peace with the Jews doesn't mean I'm a total fool."

"Is it because I'm with the Israeli delegation and sleep with the enemy? You're aware that you're sleeping with me too?"

"That's not an answer," the mapmaker said, taking her hand and giving an affectionate squeeze.

"You didn't ask a question. It was phrased as an accusation."

"I'm sure you can repeat it verbatim. I bet you could also recite the license plates of every car parked outside."

"The trick is finding the cars that stand out," she said. "It's too much to keep straight if you don't narrow them down."

"Is that an admission?"

"That's me being silly instead of upset. And, spy or no, I don't believe you're asking because of my keen eye."

"How about because you're on the National Security

team, advising? Every one of you in that group has the same hazy background in foreign service. You're the most suspect lot at the table."

"And how did you start drawing up borders and negotiating boundaries? Did you get a degree from mapmaker school? Have you formed a lot of countries before this?" She presses her toes against his. "Everyone at these negotiations has a past."

"I am, and always have been, an advocate for my people. To get anything done for them invariably means first doing something for yours. That's how I earned my seat. I'm good at wrangling Jews."

"Why did you want it—that seat?"

"Because of my deep belief that if the Palestinians are talented enough to have built your country, we can probably manage to build our own."

"Trust me, I want to see you do it. It's high time we had our country to ourselves."

"And so it begins!" he said, and started to fake tussle, which Shira was more than happy to do.

They rolled about and settled, with her straddling him, her hands pressing his shoulders to the mattress.

"So?" he said. "Are you a spy?"

"Do you think if I were that I'd be here, having sex with you? Do you honestly think I'd do that as part of my job?"

The mapmaker didn't say a word.

"Be honest," she said. "Or don't. Feel free to lie, because there is a right answer to give."

He stayed silent some more. It seemed a good way to be.

"I'm about to get very insulted," Shira said. "You really can't guess?"

She took a good grab of his carpet of chest hair and gave it an angry pull.

The mapmaker didn't say "That hurt," as they both knew it was meant to. He just gave a little yowl.

"I'd never," she said, full of a fury, the size of which he couldn't have begun to understand. Angry, and already loving him madly, she'd dropped back to his side and hugged her mapmaker tight. "Over my dead body," she'd said, for special emphasis. "That's not who I am." But she knew, as much as what she said came from the heart and felt to her as true as any truth she'd ever shared, that the woman she'd become now, she'd become solely because of what she'd done then.

If retribution was needed, on Prisoner Z's part, he finally had it. For Shira knew she was at the start of something she'd never abandon, and she knew too the impossible challenges that she and the mapmaker would face. And if anyone was to blame for this unexpected and calamitous dose of good fortune, it was undoubtedly Prisoner Z. He had set her off on a course as inevitable as the one on which she'd sent him.

She'd had more than a year to figure the mapmaker out from the time she'd first seen him, looking serious and staid, standing behind Abbas, dashing in a suit and tie. The Palestinian president was already seated along with his closest aides, when Shira had walked into the room.

She must have been looking serious herself. It was the highest-level meeting she'd ever been privy to, and easily as secret as anything she'd ever done.

There they were at Prime Minister Olmert's residence in Jerusalem, making a true and final push for peace. It was the culmination of three dozen such meets, nothing left to discuss, only to initial by the Xs on the map and for Abbas to write his name down.

She remembered how oddly tranquil it felt, stepping into that drawing room. How homey. There were cakes, and juices, sparkling water and flat. There was a bowl of clementines that she'd watched Olmert pick earlier in the day from the trees that run alongside the house.

Catching Shira watching him, he had said that such tasks calmed him before encounters of this scale.

Now she stood inside the door and observed as Olmert himself stepped forward with the map and, after a sort of half-bow, unrolled it on the table in front of Abbas.

Olmert's body man raced up, an instant's delay, with four leather paperweights, setting one on each corner, to hold it in place.

She'd looked at it, awed, and in disbelief. An independent Palestine, right there on the table. There was the end to this ancient, bloody quarrel. All Abbas needed to do was sign.

Then she looked at what they must be looking at. Not only at the map, but at Olmert, their partner in peace. This man, the General's post-stroke replacement, and, in Shira's opinion, the least prime-ministerial person she'd ever seen. With his shadow of a comb-over, and his wiry, runner's frame, and the exhausted, in-over-his-head, watery eyes. Yet, here. This map. This was truly brave. Even if the Palestinians were asking for more than Olmert was giving, he was ready to sort it out with them, and to clash with his own. There would be hell to pay on the Jewish side.

It was, she knew, very close to what they were asking. The big solutions in place. The territories marked for swap were, more or less, equitable. There was a corridor to travel from Gaza to the West Bank, a futuristic tunnel to shuttle Palestinians underground.

The tunnels, how could they then have known?

It was history in the making, if Abbas would allow history to be made. It was what she'd dreamed of being part of, once her dreams had changed.

It was then that Abbas, whispering away, pointing to this and to that, turned to glance back over his shoulder at that elegant, handsome man. It was her mapmaker, brought closer, to study the final borders that had been drawn.

She could see on his face that—this deal—he wanted to do it. That he felt, as she did, the momentousness, and fleetingness, the impossible scarcity of this peace.

He, like her, worked for those above. It was not for him to accept; it was for him to help Abbas see what he himself saw.

The mapmaker made his case. The other aides took their turns, talking that map up and down.

Abbas said he needed to think. To advise. He had to discuss it with the Jordanians. To take it to the Americans. His larger cabinet needed to be convened again before such a pact. It was more land than he was ready to lose.

It was silent, what her man did. It was the way he held himself, the way the shape of his face openly yearned. He had not said anything after his first salvo, but he now radiated a singular message that she translated as hope. Let them be two peoples living toward the future, instead of the past.

She knew this was likely her projecting, and romanticizing, and her own desperation to compromise. She wanted to take Olmert by the sleeve and announce, look at him, he is not long for power. As if Olmert knew this too, he reached into his jacket and proffered his own silver pen.

"It's only a deal if you accept it," he'd said.

Abbas looked up. Abbas did not take the pen. It was her mapmaker who reached and took it. Her mapmaker who uncapped it and held it out to his leader. He held it out for Abu Mazen, seated in front of the map of their nation. He offered it, with so much dignity, Shira thought, to the man who would not sign.

And like that, the map was whisked away. And like that the meeting was done. And when Abbas stood from his chair to go, her mapmaker dropped down on it and took up a leaf of government stationery, where he sketched out, from memory, the country that was lost. This he folded and slipped into his pocket, returning the prime minister his pen as their delegation left.

There would have to be a call in response, she was sure. There would be another round—this couldn't be everyone's bright future lost. She'd see her mapmaker again.

But Abbas's call never came, and then the invasion of Gaza was delivered instead. No one from their side wanted to talk after that war, with fourteen Israelis killed and eleven hundred Palestinians dead. After that Olmert was gone too.

There was no progress on their lack of progress for more than a year. And then, with Bibi at the helm, talking out both sides of his mouth, there was suddenly a backroom meeting in Geneva, led by the gray-haired American undersecretary whom Shira liked so much. She was a stern and clearheaded negotiator, all business, and also strong enough not to fear, in quiet intermissions, being kind.

In that parley, Shira sat across the table from the mapmaker. And their secret summit devolved into a secret rendezvous.

2014, Gaza Border (Israeli side)

It's the land of Israel, physically, that Shira loves. It's hard to explain to those who've never been, that, beyond all the flares and tracers, the pops and booms of the nightly news, it is one of the most beautiful and varied places on earth.

The desert trails in that part of the country are wildly beautiful and surprising, the waterfalls and Nubian sandstone, the great dusty mountains and their spectacular views. Makhtesh Ramon, the giant crater, is a favorite, but that is a good, long drive from there. Where she is, well, there's not so much in terms of wonder nearby. Checking the map on her phone, she's found—about an hour's walk down the road—what looks like a tiny copse of trees that the nature authority has designated as a forest. Whatever it is, it is farther from the border and outside the militarized bubble in which she currently lives. She just wants to feel alone instead of lonely, to lie down under some branches and look up through them at the sky.

Along the way, one of the old men, familiar already from the kibbutz, passes her as she trudges off on her outing, backpack slung over a shoulder, a scarf tied around her hair. He tells her, these are dangerous times to be so far from shelter.

She tells him she wants to stretch her legs and get some fresh air. He tells her right back that they have fresh air at the kibbutz, and, if she wants exercise, why not swim some laps in the pool?

Shira, unsure of why she's explaining herself, tells him she is a hiker more than a swimmer. And also, he is clearly coming back from a walk himself.

"I am old," he says. "If I die, it's sad. If you die, it's tragic."

"I'll take my chances," she says. "If a missile will find me, a missile will find me. I'd rather get blown up in nature than hiding under the bed."

He sniffles at that and takes on a wizened, salt-of-the-earth tone. "Brave talk always sounds sound," he says, "but the logic doesn't generally hold. You could also step into one of our nice fortified rooms at the sound of the sirens and not have a missile find you at all."

"I understand," she says.

"It is safer inside the gates than out. We worry over our guests."

"All right," she says. "Thanks."

Shira plugs in her earbuds and puts on the old Israeli hip-hop of the 1990s, her preferred soundtrack, a fact over which she is endlessly teased. She will concede that it's an acquired taste.

When she reaches that sad little forest, she chooses herself a lovely spot of ground, nestled between a pair of the taller trees. She takes out a water bottle, and, careful not to squish her sandwiches, she uses her backpack as a pillow, hoping to sleep for a bit. She thinks of a biblical Jacob, piling together stones. She cannot help it. Entertaining these allusions in the Holy Land, it's a condition that infects them all. She could not not-think such things if she tried.

Making her way back, feeling renewed, Shira is hardly through the front gates when she sees the man from her walk standing by the kibbutz store. She throws up her arms, as if to present herself to him, still alive—do you see, I did not get myself killed. She is proud.

But he has lost his happy demeanor. Shira, as with everyone who grew up in that country, is familiar with the look on his face.

"It is the General," he tells her, as soon as she approaches. "He's finally passed."

It shocks Shira to hear it. As much for the fact that the General was finally dead as that he was, until then, somehow still alive. Could it be that in all those years, she'd not already received that same news? Had he been with them the whole time?

She was going to say, a reflex, "I knew him personally." But it is Israel, and such claims are taken for granted. She will say that, and this venerable frontiersman will tell her that he fought in a hundred wars at the General's side. That they are brothers, or cousins, that he has given or received a kidney, that the two are childhood best friends.

She excuses herself and stumbles off from him, literally missing a step and righting herself on her way. She looks over her shoulder and, again, raises up those arms.

Is this what the world wants from her? Shira thinks. To buckle at the knees? To keen and wail?

If she does, it will be misread as grief for the General,

for whom she does not mourn. She heads toward her cottage, fighting off what has already hit her, the wave and the crash, the disoriented tumbling, as Shira is awash again in Prisoner Z.

She is stronger than this, she tells herself. She is different from other people. Let everyone judge her—as those who know her often do—but she, she will not be broken by him any more than she'd already been.

She'd seen to it that Prisoner Z was brought back on the General's orders, a traitor. What she had not seen, nor heard, was what happened to him when he'd arrived.

If the General had hung on all these years, what about the prisoner?

She had often prayed, actually prayed, that he was no longer living. For he'd never made it into the papers or surfaced on the nightly news. There was no talk in intelligence circles. There was no file that she could find, no name attached to him, no number. Her own inquiries had gone unanswered, until it was made clear she should not press anymore. And still she pressed, until it had put her on the other side of everyone's good graces. Pushed until she felt the institution pushing back, pushing her out.

She walks toward her cottage, doing the math. Twelve years. God help him. He couldn't be in limbo for so long.

And here, on the kibbutz, with the mapmaker in her heart, her diplomatic lover, who'd gotten himself trapped in Gaza for making an undiplomatic choice, she returns to her mantra for the one she'd betrayed.

Here are the things she prayed for in the weeks and months after she and the waiter zipped off in their Sea-Rider, leaving Prisoner Z sailing off toward his fate. She prayed for an accident early in the questioning. She prayed for the overzealous interrogator, and Prisoner Z's broken neck. She hoped he'd been drowned in a bucket, or that his heart had given out from the stress. She wished upon wishing that Prisoner Z had attempted escape, tasting some dream of false freedom, never feeling the bullet to the back of the head.

2014, Lifta

Change. It fixes Ruthi with a mix of wonder and dread. She has taken her son's advice—a first. She'd watered her plants and put on her comfortable shoes. She'd headed down into her neighborhood, not to shop or run errands, but, simply, to be.

The old city is what she misses, on her walk. Not the one of Turkish rampart and holy site, of Wailing Wall and golden dome. She means the old-new Jerusalem, the plain, dusty, wonderful hamlet of her childhood, where a person could live simply. Dignified and poor.

Everywhere she goes, she passes towering new buildings, and Ruthi knows when she happens on a gap and the vistas open up, she'll see hilltop after hilltop covered with houses where once there were terraces, the thin-trunked forests of the valleys filled with villas and ribbons of newly paved road. All covering the places Ruthi and her friends used to hike when she was a girl. They'd go off hunting treasure that, on rare days, they'd actually find. Ancient coins and bits of pearled glass, picked like seashells from between the flagstones of Roman byways. Often, they'd tumble down the path into Lifta, and, if no boys were lurking, they'd jump into the spring in their underwear and then dry out in the sun. They'd play hide-and-seek in the abandoned houses in that husk of an Arab village at the city's mouth.

Why not? is what Ruthi thinks. How long has it been?

Ruthi turns herself toward the entrance to the city. She walks slowly, twisting down toward the *trampiada* where the soldiers point fingers to the ground hitchhiking rides, and the Hassidim do the same, each in the uniform of his tribe.

Feeling naughty, and girlish again, she steps off the road and follows that same steep path into the gorge, escaping back to a time she sorely missed.

It is as it was. The Arab houses still stand. And she pictures—a flash of memory—the speed with which the gazelles raced off when she and her friends would arrive. Religious girls, they used to pretend—hardly a reach—that this green spring-fed place was the Garden of Eden, and that they were the first ever to walk the world, the houses erased from their view.

The General, always with her when he was living, had not moved far since he'd gone. She stands at the foot of the pool in which she'd swum, and she remembers one of the numberless late nights at the General's official residence, all but her, and his bodyguards, sent home.

He had come in from the patio to find her in his office, closing things up for the day. "There is a visitor coming," he'd said. "It's very last-minute, I know, but I don't want to wake anyone to cook."

She had scolded him, saying, "If you are asking me something, please ask it."

"Could you put something together—as a favor to me? Something simple for a guest."

"It will have to be," she'd said, frustrated, as she knew the pantry was as empty as it ever got, a big order coming the next day.

She'd gone through the kitchen, and there were eggs and peppers and some vegetables in cans. There were fruits and a watermelon, and some cheeses and a good loaf of bread. There was a tub of hummus. And she knew she could make do.

She started on a shakshuka, and warmed day-old burrekas, and began chopping cucumbers for a nice Israeli salad, only sorry she had no parsley or mint to put on top.

She'd set out pickles and olives, and if the meal were to have a theme, she'd call it a late-night breakfast spread.

While she was still cooking, in came the General, and with him, she could not believe it, was Arafat at his side.

There he stood in his uniform and his famous kaffiyeh, the tail of that scarf set carefully in the shape of greater Israel, Palestine resting on his lapel. She rarely felt silenced, but him—she'd never met Arafat before.

The General, in good spirits, made introductions. He'd said, "My favorite enemy has stopped by for a chat."

Then Arafat had addressed her, in that high voice she'd only ever heard on the radio and TV. It sounded just the same, coming—nice to meet you—from the man's full lips.

The men did not move out to the General's office or the dining room, or to sit in the center patio, where so many visitors were entertained. They sat down at the kitchen table, and the General said, "Ruthi, enough time has been wasted by both sides. We're here to make progress. And where more efficient than the kitchen to set out food?"

She'd offered to excuse herself, before the rest of the cooking was done.

The General, seeming sincerely hospitable, insisted she stay.

And so she'd remained, cooking and serving, hurrying back and forth, shuttling the finished plates from the counter, pouring drinks and refreshing. A fly on the wall.

It was not business, not politics, not the future of the peoples that they were yet discussing. While she ladled shakshuka, the two reminisced over all the times they'd tried to kill each other and failed, all their accidents and close calls, all the times they did not die.

"When my plane crashed in the desert," Arafat said, "and I walked away."

"When I was a young man, shot in the gut at Latrun."

"When you had me in your sniper sights in Beirut."

"You know about that?" the General had said, beaming.

"I have seen the photo. And if I did, you must have wanted me to see it too."

"We should have pulled the trigger."

"It would have saved you the price of this dinner," Arafat said, as he took a pickle from the dish. "Why didn't you? I've always wanted to know. Russian pressure? American?"

"Only because it wouldn't have been right," the General said. "The Devil so enjoys having us both around."

She was good at reading her boss. She continued to dawdle in the kitchen, puttering around, helping contribute to that informal tone. She listened as they moved on to the point that seemed to have spurred this late-night meet.

The Palestinians are willing to sacrifice many things, Arafat had said, but they must at least be able to save face. On the right of return, they need a symbol. Not just a state outside those borders, but a return to someplace within.

What easier population for the Israelis to absorb, and what better place to rebuild than the tiny village of Lifta, a gem over which their broken hearts never mend?

And what else should Ruthi remember as she stands

among those vacant stone houses, climbing the gorge on both sides?

Toward the end of that meeting, toward the end of that meal, Ruthi approached with feta and watermelon on a serving platter. Sweet and salty, a favorite of the General's until the start of his endless end.

He'd openly balked at Arafat's request. The General would swap more territory, closer in. He would talk about taking more refugees, a bolder number, in a place farther away.

And, just then, Arafat turned to her. He'd touched a hand to her arm, as if she'd been part of the conversation the whole time. "Is it not beautiful, our Lifta? You must have seen?"

"I have," she'd said, and she'd answered not in Hebrew or English, but Arabic, and Arafat had smiled. "It is beautiful," she'd said, and set the platter down before him.

It was this that they then argued. Repeating how willing they both were to compromise, they both, on this, stood fast.

"A right of return," Arafat had said. "A few houses, already built, standing empty at the bottom of Jerusalem, low down. You will have the advantage of height and position should it ever again come to war."

"It is not the bottom of the city, but the top of Israel, and you know that. Jerusalem is the Jewish head, and Lifta sits at its throat." The General put his finger to his neck and did not need, for effect, to pull it across.

"Give us that," Arafat said. "We should not have to ask for what's ours."

"If it were yours already," the General had said, "you would not have to come asking at my door."

2014, Gaza Border (Israeli side)

The care one must take in a relationship not to say the things that won't go away. She had insulted her love grievously the last time she'd seen him face-to-face.

They were having dinner in Amsterdam when he'd told her he was flying straight from there to Gaza. He was being sent as an emissary to bury the hatchet and reunite the Palestinian people. He would broker a different kind of deal from the one to which they'd dedicated their lives. The mapmaker was going to wrangle a lasting peace between Palestinians and Palestinians, between Fatah and Hamas.

When he'd said it, she'd used the *T* word, which was something, between them, that they did not do. She'd been worried for his safety on any number of fronts. And she'd maybe called Hamas—all of them, political and military bunched up together, she'd maybe called them "terrorists" outright.

What if things went bad? is all she'd been trying to say. What if he was arrested by his hosts and locked in one of their prisons? What if Israel did not let him leave. "They do not want Hamas as a third negotiating partner," she'd told him. "It's fire that you're playing with, they won't take it well."

She could still feel the anger of it, the coiled force of him.

Then he'd said, in response, composed again, " 'They,' as you know, are 'you.' "

She did know that, very well. She was a former spy, at present on the National Security team, championing the treaty they never signed. And that's why she was giving him her vulgar advice.

She'd been right, of course. They both had been, each in their way. As, when he'd finished the first round of his business and tried to leave, the Israelis had laughed at his diplomatic status and taken his papers away. They'd kept him in Gaza until this very day. But her man! Her mapmaker, he got things done. They'd kept him in and he'd kept working and Israel got just the opposite of what they'd intended—as happens with everything in the region. *Hafuh al hafuh,* was the rule.

It had taken a year, a year of them apart, a year of him pushing day and night. He'd finally executed his Palestinian unity government. And what good would that progress do in Gaza, when Israel—when the "they" that was "she"— would come in and smash apart whatever was built?

On the way back from dinner, she'd walked alongside him, letting him stew. She was trying to wait out one of his measured responses as it traveled the epic distance from deep inside his reserved, reticent self.

The mapmaker finally stopped and turned to face her. She knew he didn't notice such things, but they were in the middle of a little bridge. He was going to say something grim, she was sure, and he did not at all notice that the spot was more suited for one of them to propose.

"I'm going either way," he'd said. "With your support or without."

It is the bridge that she pictures, missing him, solitary in her cottage. And it is what he'd said then that she holds on to, though she'd initially been unsure of what he'd meant.

"Our issues," the mapmaker had told her, looking as tearful as she'd ever seen. "They're insurmountable, far beyond hope."

"Yours and mine?" she'd asked, already grieving. "Or yours and ours?"

"I don't know if it's worth trying any longer," he'd said, and she followed his gaze across the mirrored black surface of the canal.

Teetering on the frantic, she'd said, "Trying with *me,* or trying with *us*? Peoples or persons, which do you mean? On what do you quit?"

"On 'you,' the Israelis," he'd said, taking her hands. He'd not even entertained the option she'd feared. "With Bibi back, we'll never move ahead, and he will never lose power. It is time for us to join forces—Fatah and Hamas. To forget about Israel and achieve unity for ourselves. Maybe it's best if we fix our own house first."

Even just thinking it now, she is ashamed at how deeply she'd been relieved. It was so selfish a thing to hang on to. How happy she'd been to hear her mapmaker still loved her, and it was only a future for the two peoples, together, that he'd thought was lost.

2014, Black Site (Negev Desert)

He paces too much and bites his nails too low. He's stopped eating his food, and he's taken to banging his head against the wall—not hard, not hard, is what he tells the guard. It looks worse on the camera, but when it gets this hot, when the seasons bring us here, the tapping on the cinder blocks, it is cooling.

The guard, Prisoner Z thinks, the guard must be concerned. For the guard gets the pills, stronger and better, and on the regular. Prisoner Z imagines it's because, though the pacing has lessened, it's more that he's been having some problems standing up.

It's not the guard's business, Prisoner Z feels, and he has been denying. But the guard keeps coming and saying, "Stand up, then, if you can do it." And when Prisoner Z tries, the room sets to spinning. There is a new thing, a vertigo, that he's never had before.

He is fine on the mattress. And fine on the floor. But the guard won't leave off him. Prisoner Z tells him it's an inner ear infection or a burst eardrum, that, maybe once, he'd hit too hard against that wall.

The guard, who is not a doctor by any means, tells him, "I think it's because you're losing your mind."

Prisoner Z hates when the guard is right, but after a tranquilizer or two, the room slows for Prisoner Z and then stops. Sometimes, Prisoner Z crawls to the toilet anyway and props himself up with a shaky hand, so the cameras don't betray him and give that torturer the satisfaction.

More and more frequently it is so bad that there is, anyway, no satisfaction to be had, and that's when the guard would rush in.

"Breathe," he would say, "you're having a panic attack."

"I'm fine," Prisoner Z would tell him, while looking very not fine.

On those occasions the guard might hold Prisoner Z, he might rock him if the motion didn't make things worse, or rub Prisoner Z's back in big circles.

"Try and cry," the guard would whisper. "This is instead of that. It's not real. Try and be sad and you'll feel better."

"Fuck," Prisoner Z might also say, between breaths. And trying harder, "Go, and fuck, yourself."

"Okay, I will," the guard would promise, with the same serene intonation. "Right after you calm down, I'll go fuck myself good. That's right. That's excellent. Be angry. That'll help. Angry is as good as sad."

When Prisoner Z would start to calm, when he'd get his usual color, or lack of color, back—a clamminess, still, to everything about him—after order was marginally restored, neither would admit what had passed between them.

This very last time, holding Prisoner Z's dizzy head in his lap, the guard had gone as far as either dared at addressing it. He had posed a question to Prisoner Z, to himself, to the cameras, as if confronting a power higher than them both.

How, oh how, has it come to this?

He had asked it, appearing, to Prisoner Z, reflective—not his usual dummy's face.

And lying there in his cell, long after the guard has gone, Prisoner Z has dedicated many hours to formulating an answer.

It would be easy to say that it was because of the waitress or Sander, the Huguenot waiter or Farid. But he does not blame the spying or counter-spying, not the betraying of country, nor his taking part in an operation that killed so many kids. It wasn't his training to which he traced it, nor to his recruitment at Hebrew University by a friend who had handed him a number and said, "Reach out, if you want to contribute in a special way."

How it had come to this, Prisoner Z felt, had been set so very early. His Jerusalem, his Israel, his end. He'd been given it so long ago, back in suburbia, back in America, a birthright spoon-fed to him in his Jewish day school classroom, a little boy, with a heavy prayer book and a yarmulke, like a soup bowl turned over and resting atop his head.

It is second grade, and they are running—the children—with their arms outspread. They are flying. The desks are pushed together, the teacher's orders, their lovely eighteen-year-old teacher, who would soon get pregnant and disappear.

They know enough, the boys and girls, to love this black-haired lady, whose even more black, more beautiful hair peeks out from under her wig as she pushes the big desk, the teacher's desk, toward theirs. She dresses modestly, but there is no modest when you are a beautiful raven-haired eighteen-year-old second-grade teacher, flushed from trying to get pregnant in all your free time.

Their love for her was different from what they felt for the others. It was marrying-love, and wanting-to-be-her-love, and it was youthful energetic teacher love, and they would do anything for her—anything at all. So when, after morning prayer, after marching into the room with their big green *siddurim* and taking their seats, when she'd stood, and jutted out her bottom jaw and blown the hair from her eyes, when she'd said, "Up, up," and raised her hands, raising the class so easily with them, Prisoner Z is no longer sure if she'd actually spoken the "Up, up" at all.

"We are going somewhere and we are late," is what she says.

"Where are we going?" asks Batya, whose English name is Beth.

A smile from the teacher, a glimmer to the eye. "We are going, my little *Yidelach,* to Yerushalyim. We are flying, right now, to Israel. The *Moshiach* is coming and we need to get there. We need to help welcome him in." And the hands again are waving, and we are all already following. "Now push! Push the desks together so we can get up into the sky."

And when those desks are all together, a circle around the room, the teacher takes one of our tiny chairs, raising her skirt so we can see her ankle swathed in her scratchy gray tights. She places a foot on the seat of that chair and then climbs onto those child-sized desks. A teacher! A teacher standing on a desk! It is glorious.

She bends a bit at the knees and leans her head forward. The teacher then spreads her arms wide. She says, "I am on an airplane. I *am* an airplane. We are all flying to Israel together, to make aliyah. We are headed to Jerusalem. We must hurry, hurry, a long flight and the Messiah is already on his way."

And she takes off like that, flying from desk to desk around the room. Tilting her beautiful, covered arms on the turns.

"Come," she says. "Come. You do not want to be left in *galus*, forgotten in this Egypt, when the Messiah comes. Our country awaits." And it is roly-poly Bentzi who is first up, and then Meir Aryeh follows, flashing his monkey grin, there are Devorah and Yocheved, Susan and Zev. And then I am on the chair—Prisoner Z feels himself rising. But with all those arms tilting, and everyone running and howling and flying, I'm too afraid to join. And suddenly I am grabbed and suddenly I am lifted, the teacher has got me, she is holding me, and she sets me down in motion—and that is love, and that is care.

She holds on until my feet are moving and my arms spreading, until I too, I feel it, until I am looking down at the classroom below, down at New York, at America, until it all looks like desert and all looks like wasteland, nothing but the emptiness that is the whole world outside what God gave us.

2014, Gaza Border (Israeli side)

She and the mapmaker were like teenagers in their attachment. They had so many games they played on their furtive weekends away. One was a game she'd lifted from her parents, her Italian-Israeli father and her Moroccan-Israeli mother, a way to understand the different worldviews from which they came.

They would, she and her mapmaker, name the singular people who'd, in their belief, changed history. Not the Stalins and the Hitlers, but the regular actors who'd altered the course of the planet.

When they'd first played, she'd said, "Yigal Amir," for having murdered Rabin and, in her opinion, single-handedly torpedoing the peace for which they fought.

He'd said, "Baruch Goldstein," for his massacre at the Tomb of the Patriarchs, which, in the mapmaker's opinion, had set off the wave of violence that landed them in this woebegone state.

She'd liked the game better when her parents had played it. She was upset, already, at the start.

"I'd argue that point," she'd said.

"You argue every point."

She'd sat up to better face him, prone, as they perpetually were, in a hotel's king-size bed. He'd stared at her over his glasses as he closed, around his finger, the book she wouldn't let him read.

"We can't both pick Israelis, is what I mean," she'd said. "It's not fair."

"Isn't it? It's your game."

"Pick someone else. I have a long list of Palestinians you can borrow."

"No, no," he'd said. "I'll come up with a new one myself." And he'd thought and he'd thought and he'd said, "Katherine Harris."

Shira had absolutely no idea who that was.

"The American woman," her mapmaker had said. "From the election in 2000. She was the one in Florida, where they were counting the holes in the papers. Or the half-holes not punched out. She is the one who decided to award that state to George Bush, even though she was tied to his campaign. Partisan. Political. Corrupted. From her, all the dominoes fall. Through Iraq. Through Syria. Toppling over Palestine, knocking it down. Who knows where the chain ends, maybe with the end of all that we know?"

Shira had to process that for a good long while.

"Wow," she'd said. "That is a crazy pick and exactly how you play. You are the winner of round one. I admit defeat."

He was proud, and they'd kissed, a peck on the lips—it was that kind of night—and each had rolled the other way. The mapmaker, dropping his book to the floor, clicked off the lights.

Stepping outside her cottage into that blistering morning

sun, Shira regrets every kiss that could have been a long one. She regrets every bit of intimacy shortchanged. The rules of that game could so easily have been altered. They could have named not the singular folk who'd changed history, but those individuals who'd forever changed them.

If she were playing the game of her own life, she knows, it's because of Prisoner Z that she found herself right where she was—living on this kibbutz under false pretense, waiting for her Palestinian love to send her a signal, ready to take an insane chance to see her mapmaker one more time.

The paths of life, they are infinite in their weaving.

She walks east that day, hitching a ride for most of the way, wanting to wander around the Shokeda Forest. The summer heat is as brutal as ever, and she already knew, on her way over, that she'd missed the flowing fields of red anemone by months.

It's a nice ramble anyway. There are some handsome pines growing in the park and a lot of eucalyptus and an ancient-looking tamarisk here and there.

In the past, she'd driven down south at the far edge of winter, when everything in these parts blooms. Shira had once been lucky enough to be in the Negev after a good rain. She'd caught the desert in full blossom. All those flowers hiding in the sand.

When the sirens sound, she decides they are coming from a distance. It is only as they scream on that Shira understands the noise isn't reaching her from one of the big cities but coming from the kibbutzim and moshavim nearby.

She understands she and those trees are quite possibly under fire. She lies down where she stands, and she puts her trusty daypack over her head for a bit of useless protection. She presses her face into the ground.

She can feel it, the pressure, a salvo striking close, those drunken, screwy missiles headed her way.

It would serve her right, this fate. She's so far off course from what she'd imagined her life would be, it would make sense for her to be killed by a random missile meant to miss everything and everyone and bury itself in the dirt.

It is incredibly forbidding, the strike and boom. Shira wonders if she will survive the assault as she waits for the last siren's wail. She stays motionless, the bag atop her head, the earth gritty in her teeth. Even with her mouth closed it makes its way in. So great is the strength of impact.

How often had they whispered on the phone, talking deep into the night, she, with her head buried under the pillows, feeling somehow swaddled, while wishing the mapmaker were actually at her side.

She'd say things like "Could you come by boat?" "Can you paraglide?" "What about a scuba tank?" "What if I walked across the Sinai Desert?" "What if I stole a helicopter, like they do in the movies?" "What if I get the president of the United States involved?"

To this game, the mapmaker never played along. If there were a way to get out, he'd have found it.

Yet, despite all the challenges, their dual and exhausting obsessions with their peoples' plights, and the endless pressures the distance put upon them, their devotion only grew. "And why shouldn't it?" she'd ask him. Of all the outrageous things in which anyone had ever believed, the undoable dreams of oceans crossed, and mountains climbed, of men put on the moon, why couldn't the triumph of their relationship be one?

"Yes," he'd say. "They've cloned sheep."

"And transplanted a human face!"

"I saw a dog on the Internet that sounds like it's saying 'Hello.' It's very clear."

"Miracles abound," she'd say. "Why can't us together be another?"

Then they'd tick through the great and legendary loves, separated by history and reunited against all odds.

For so long it had gone on like that, the calls always closing with the mapmaker mum and Shira asking, "If you can't get out, and I can't get in, what do we do?"

There was no answer to give. There was no more love to be claimed than the great love they shared, no more missing to privately suffer or, between them, to lament. Then one day, he called early while she sat reading at a café in Florentin. Before she'd uttered "Hello," he'd said to her, "I would die to see you. I would."

"That's romantic," was her response.

"I would literally die to see you, is what I mean."

"I would too," she'd said.

"Would you?"

"I would," she'd said.

"I couldn't handle that."

"It's my right, as it is yours. If you respect me."

"Then ask me your question," he'd said. "The same one as always."

She did. She knew just which question he meant.

"If you can't get out and I can't get in?"

And he'd answered.

"We meet in tl.e middle," is what the mapmaker said.

"What does that mean?"

"It means the tunnels. It means meeting underground. A rendezvous."

Shira stepped outside. She'd smiled and tossed back her hair, making the face she would make if he were sitting across from her, gazing.

"Okay," she says. "Sure."

"I'm serious."

"For one, that's insane. And for two, the tunnels are closed. The tunnels to Egypt are done."

"I said, 'meet in the middle.' Egypt is not in between us. Egypt is on the other side."

"So what's the middle?"

"There are other tunnels."

"To where?"

"Tunnels between Gaza and Israel. Military tunnels. Tunnels that run from your door to mine."

Shira remembered how she'd looked around then. She'd made a full spin, to see who might be near.

"Are you serious?"

"You prepare for the next war, as do we. You must know they are there."

"I don't think we do."

"Let's meet."

"In a tunnel?"

"Yes."

"Don't I have to tell someone? They need to know."

"They do not need to know."

"People could die. They will die."

"Honestly, if something happens, whose people will be the ones dying? You think our tunnels will turn the tide? That they'll open like a giant mouth and swallow Israel whole? What they'll do is make martyrs to inspire new martyrs. Do you think Jerusalem will fall from a hole in the dirt?"

"What if they grab another soldier? What if they make it to the nearest kibbutz?"

"I didn't ask you about what happens in war. I'm asking if you want to have dinner with me."

"In a tunnel? Underground?"

"You don't have to make it sound so dreary."

"What other way is there?"

"Candlelight. A white tablecloth. For you, a bottle of wine."

"That does sound better."

"Yes, it does. Just picture it, the two of us in no-man's-land, on the blurry line beneath neither country. Me and you, eating together between worlds. A dinner at the center of the earth."

2014, Gaza Border (Palestinian side)

The mapmaker sits in an office that is not an office, but the living room of this very hulking man's house. His host, bald-headed and jowled, looks to be strong as an ox, broad in the chest, big in the belly, with a forearm the size of the map-maker's leg.

His host keeps excusing himself to step out into the alley, where he has coals heating up on the grill. When he comes back, he barely sits down before he's off to the kitchen. Each time he goes he says, "Marinating," in place of "Excuse me," and then returns licking the same finger, which he must be using to test the taste of something good.

A behemoth of a flat screen is mounted on the wall play-ing kids' shows at a setting that the mapmaker finds to be dis-tractingly loud. There are toys on the floor, but no children to be seen.

A man introduced as "my idiot son," who is probably thirty or thirty-five, leans against the wall opposite the TV, smoking a cigarette and staring at the mapmaker, suspect and cold.

When his host finally settles in across the table, he tells

that big, strong, suspect-of-the-mapmaker-looking son to go fan those coals.

To the mapmaker, he says, "It's an honor to have you in my home. I thank you for your service to our nation."

Modest, the mapmaker replies that the honor is his and then says, "They say you are the best."

"At what? At grilling? If so, that's demonstrably true."

"It's tunneling that I mean," the mapmaker says, as frank as can be. "At engineering the routes, and smuggling things through them, they say you are without equal."

The man leans forward and points a threatening, fat finger. "You wouldn't happen to be a stool pigeon, who's going to get me killed by an Israeli drone if I accept the compliment?"

"Would those who put us in touch have sent me, if so?"

The man considers his guest and, after some contemplation, says, "In my heyday, I did it all. Things you wouldn't believe."

"Yes," the mapmaker says, "so they say."

"What did you hear, if you know already?"

"They credit you with getting anything needed in, and anyone who needed, out. They say you brought enough cement for a skyscraper, enough steel for a bridge—or for a thousand thousand missiles to fight those who oppress us. They say you brought food for the hungry, and medicines for the sickly."

"Not just the food," the man says. "The beasts the food comes from. I've brought goats and chickens, and more cows than I can count."

"That must be something to see, underground."

From the doorway, the son, who has reappeared, says, "It's not the craziest by far."

"What's the craziest, by far, then?" the mapmaker asks, ingratiating himself.

Idiot or no, the father looks to his son, before deciding whether to talk. Then he says, "A rich customer wanted a classic car. A Mercedes 300SL, with the gull-wing doors," and, as if by reflex, both father's and son's arms float up, to illustrate. "But it's too wide for the widest tunnel. There's no way to get it through. I try and figure for weeks, how to dig wider, and keep it from caving. Then it hits me. A show I saw once, about the Empire State Building, in New York. To make publicity for the Ford Motor Company, they wanted to put a Mustang on the roof as a stunt. But how to get it a hundred stories high? You can't drive it up the stairs."

"Okay," the mapmaker says.

"What they did is, they cut it into pieces, and brought it in the elevators, and reassembled it on top. And I thought, what's the difference, straight up or straight across? If it will fit through the tunnel in pieces, why not?" He sits back then and crosses his arms on his chest, as if to be admired. "We got it through with centimeters to spare."

"I bet you got rich off it too."

The man coughs a cough that sounds to be a mix of pneumonia and laughter.

"I barely broke even. But, like the Ford people, one cannot put a price on good publicity. Even black marketeers need to spread the word."

"Well, it worked. I've brought my very special request to you."

"And I'd have loved to hear it, but the Egyptians have destroyed everything. We'd just finished a new route too. It had automated tracks, little flatbeds running off of motorcycle engines, zipping along."

"I'm sorry for your loss," the mapmaker says, as if there'd been a death in the family.

"Yes. Like all Gaza's tunnel millionaires, I've been forcibly retired."

"We've only just met," the mapmaker says, "but you don't seem the type to give up and just sit around."

His host taps at his temple, squinting an eye. "I'm busy here, working on the next wave. Whether it's another five years or ten before they ease up, I'll be ready when there's opportunity below. I'm designing a micro-tunnel, using PVC pipe. Invisible to sonar, unbombable. And the trick? We pressurize it. You know? We make it pneumatic and shoot capsules back and forth. Small stuff. Money. Pharmaceuticals. We'll whip things back and forth, faster than running to the store."

"Ingenious."

"Not my invention. I've been following the Mexicans, online. They do amazing things beneath the United States borders. My job is not to innovate, it is to evolve."

The mapmaker clears his throat. "If it's evolution you're after, I've come to ask for something never done before."

"If only I could help," he says, offering a compassionate frown. His jowls make an impressive drop.

"Is it all right if I choose not to believe you?" the mapmaker says.

"Believe what you want. Everyone does these days." He shrugs. "Tell me, though, if I were still in business, what might you want me to move?"

"A woman," the mapmaker says.

"That's why you come to me, full of drama? You want to get some cousin into Egypt. Why didn't you say? If she isn't on the lists, if her record is clean, we still do some medical tourism."

"Bribery and forgery aren't technically smuggling," the son says. "For us, medical tourism, it's kind of a sideline."

The father turns to his son, his mood changing in a flash. "How are you still here? What color are my coals?"

The son disappears into the kitchen and then outside with a tray of meat. When the door closes behind him, the mapmaker says, "The woman, she's not my relative. And I said I needed help smuggling, but it's not out that I'm after."

"Either direction, it's the same issue. The routes are shut. The tunnels flooded and caved in."

"That I know," the mapmaker says. "But it's from Israel that I mean. It's those tunnels that I'm after."

The mapmaker's host turns bright red. He jumps up, grabbing the remote, and shuts off the TV. His son pokes his head in and he bellows at him, telling him to keep by the grill and keep that door closed.

Turning back to the mapmaker, he says, full of fury, "What are you talking about? No such tunnels exist."

"I want to bring a woman in. A Jew. From Israel."

"A death sentence! For you, for her, and for me, probably just for discussing it."

"I told her the same," the mapmaker says, fully agreeing. "Which is why I don't want to bring her all the way in. I just want to meet her, underneath."

"What do you mean—meet her underneath?"

"For a date. In whatever passage you can arrange."

"This is all about a date? You want to fuck someone in a tunnel?"

"Careful," the mapmaker says. "But, yes, it is a date. Think of it like a rental. I want to rent out a tunnel to Israel for an evening."

The man goes over to a side table and hunts around in a drawer. He comes up with a pack of cigarettes, the matches tucked in it. He lights one for himself and manically puffs away.

When the nicotine hits and he can speak again, he says, "True madness." And then he says, "Why in the world do you think there's a tunnel to Israel?"

"For the next war. The one that will surely come. I know that they're there. And I know you're the one who puts them there."

The man goes to the door. He locks it and leans his back against it.

"Let us pretend," he says, "that instead of a cigarette, it's a gun that I dug out of that drawer." Aiming the cigarette at the mapmaker's face, he says, "Let's act as if it's a nine-millimeter pistol that I am pointing between your eyes."

"All right," the mapmaker says.

"Do you feel it?"

The mapmaker responds with a look, not daring to nod.

"Good," he says. "Now, tell me. Is this some fake, double-cross-type fuckery that you bring us? Because I've let you into my home, and told you my business, and am now going to feed you the food I have so passionately prepared."

The mapmaker, careful not to panic, and also careful not to insult by looking too calm, says, "This is a real and honest request."

"Because the kind of thing you're asking touches on some heavy, ordered from the top, paid for by Iran type of shit. These tunnels that don't exist are as serious as things get."

"What I ask is personal and private. I'm not trying to sneak out myself, or embark on a suicide mission. I am trying to see the woman I adore."

"Don't you know she must be a spy who wants to find the tunnel entrance and maybe kill you inside it?"

The mapmaker says, "I promise she isn't," which is far simpler, in the moment, than adding, "not anymore."

"And you're not ratting us out like Sheikh Yousef's boy?" Here he spits on the floor, a curse on that turncoat.

"No," the mapmaker says.

"To bring a Jew into the tunnels—a woman—it is the worst of their bogeyman fears."

"Again, I'm not taking her anywhere. She, as much as me, wants to meet. We'd like to have dinner. To be in the same place, to touch." It is as critical an instant as any he'd faced. How to say it, how to tell him, that she was the one for whom he hadn't known he was waiting. That providence had made the least likely person the one he couldn't live without. The mapmaker says, "I am a man trapped. And in love."

His host, the mapmaker can see, can neither believe what he's hearing nor what he is considering himself. For he shakes his head, and circles the room, he coughs again, and laughs again, and stops to size up the mapmaker more than once. He puffs at that cigarette and jabs a finger the mapmaker's way.

"Okay," he says. "Yes, all right. I'll do it."

"Okay? For real?"

He gives another giant, broad-bodied shrug.

"Who can fight love?"

2014, Black Site (Negev Desert)

The guard brings the prisoner his favorites, a falafel in a lafa, a bottle of Eagle Malt, and—an American treat—a bag of ice. He is hoping his prisoner will eat. The guard takes a second bottle from his backpack, this one vodka that he'd frozen. It pours like syrup into the paper cups.

While Prisoner Z sets up the board he says, "You're really spoiling me today. Our best preholiday party yet."

"There's something else!" the guard says, excitement in his voice.

Prisoner Z smiles faintly, already knowing. Every gloomy year in that cell, the guard marks one of the three big holidays with a present. The same gift, every time.

The guard pulls it out, wrapped. Prisoner Z says thanks and sets it, in its festive paper, aside.

They play backgammon. They drink until they're more or less soused. The prisoner acting as close to himself as he has in a while.

As the guard leaves, the prisoner asks, "Is it rude that I didn't open it? I can open it in front of you if you want."

"No, no. To open it will make us both shy."

The guard tosses the trash in the plastic bag he'd brought the lafa in. He stows the vodka and the backgammon board in his knapsack and, reaching over to the peg by the shower, removes Prisoner Z's worn robe.

"I'll just take the old one," he says, standing by the open door.

"Do," Prisoner Z says. "And enjoy the holiday with your mother. I imagine I'll be here when you get back."

"I imagine so," the guard says, and locks that heavy door behind him.

Feeling too tipsy to drive and with two more hours to his shift, he sits in the dark of the supply closet that has been, for all these years, his office.

He taps at his keyboard and moves around the mouse, choosing which of the pictures to enlarge.

It's the camera over the entrance that offers the best angle. It's as if the guard, himself, floats above the prisoner in the cell, staring down.

He watches his friend sitting alone on the bed. The way the prisoner's shoulders are rolled forward, the guard wonders if the prisoner is quietly crying, or simply considering his toes.

Prisoner Z straightens up then. He reaches over and takes the package, in its jolly wrapping. He undoes the paper carefully, as if he might reuse it for someone else's gift.

The guard can see that the prisoner is, for once, laughing. It is his annual robe.

Prisoner Z holds it up, a new color. He stands up, puts it on, and, pulling the two lapels closed, he reaches—

Prisoner Z reaches down and reaches back, a habit with robes that he's surprised he has not lost. Or is it that he subconsciously absorbed what he had not before consciously noticed, but—it cannot be.

The belt is on the robe. The belt is still there, hanging through its loops.

Prisoner Z first tries tying it loosely around his waist. He undoes the belt and reties it, more snugly.

He simply cannot imagine that the guard has forgotten.

The guard stays there, in the dark, at his desk and watches Prisoner Z tie and untie, tie and untie. And then slip the sash from its loops.

Prisoner Z holds it there, strung across both palms, its length hanging down on both sides.

The guard watches as the prisoner, his friend, slowly raises his eyes and looks right into the camera above the door. They know each other well.

From the guard's perspective, it's as if there's nothing between them, no screen and no camera, no walls or metal doors, no numbers rolling and rolling in waves of code to build the picture that he sees. For the guard, it is simply and purely the prisoner looking up at him, mournful, staring right into his eyes.

It is a face of confusion, and a face of understanding. What the guard cannot tell is if it's also a look of thanks.

But this the guard will leave for himself to wonder over. There are some things a friend should not see.

Easy as that, his prisoner steps toward the shower, into the one space to which the camera he monitors is blind. The guard does not change views. Instead, he reaches around to the backs of the displays and clicks them off for the first time in years. So rarely is this done, it is as if the devices themselves have their own capacity for shock. They make a sort of strange, crackling sigh as the electricity empties out.

With his foot, the guard flips the glowing switch to the power strip on the floor, and then, fiddling with the computer tower, he pinches the Ethernet cable from its port.

These actions, of course, do not serve to undo the moment itself. They stop time for the guard but do not, in the prisoner's cell, slow anything down.

All the guard has done is shut his own eyes in three different ways. What he's done is deny a record of a certain amount of time, though the cameras are still there looking, even if they can no longer share what it is they see.

It's that notion the guard thinks about on his drive home for the holidays, racing to beat the traffic where it jams up by Motsa. He's supposed to have dinner on the balcony with his mother, and, for that, he does not want to be late.

2014, Limbo

The General stands atop the Temple Mount, where the Holy of Holies once stood. He waits for a sign from God, a sign to make peace or make war, to make anything more than another tired political point.

He receives no signals, no auguries, no omens, no wonders. It was right here, in this place, that Abraham, lucky man, was sent a ram to offer in Isaac's stead. The General himself was not, as a father, spared.

Listening, he suddenly hears it, the sound of that tune. That voice singing the song he so loves. He looks to the force that surrounds him, a thousand strong, to see if anyone else hears the same.

The men do not show it. And the General is confused, for each of those assembled now wears the face of his lost son.

The sons of Israel, they are all his.

Up here on this sacred, contested site, the General finally makes sense of it. He looks straight up to Heaven, and then out to the Valley of Hinnom, over the Old City walls, where the perverse kings of Judah sacrificed their own.

The General knows—warrior, peacemaker, murderer,

saint—that his time on this earth must be up. He stands there listening to that voice, then to the sound of the needle as that silent record spins.

The General, who does not panic, who never hid from death, does not worry even now.

He looks one more time out over his mighty troops, out over his united Jerusalem, out to the Judean Hills that hold all of the history that to him ever mattered. The General stands on that high point, in God's beloved city, the one He held above the waters when He flooded, in anger, the world.

2014, Down Under and In Between

Shells hit, and missiles strike, the walls around them shake. The tunnel, solid as it is, well built as it is, withstands. The part Shira can see, as if they're in the belly of a serpent, ripples up ahead. She wonders if the whole thing might slither away with the two of them inside. The seams of the concrete sections rain down dust and then settle like old bones, when the moments of quiet come.

The lanterns stay lit. The candle he promised holds its place on the table and still burns.

The mapmaker, as if they don't have a care in the world, pours her more wine, my love, my sweet.

"We have picked a bad night for our dinner," he says.

"Unless, for us, it's the best."

Always positive, always seeing the bright side, this is why he has fallen for her. Though he can't not ask, "How could that possibly be?"

"Maybe our horrible, self-destructive peoples, maybe our vacillating cowardly nations, maybe our brave soldiers always looking to die, maybe tonight they'll finally all kill each other and see this conflict done. It is time, Old World style, to fly the bloodred flag of no quarter and fight until no one is left."

"And how would that be to our advantage?" he asks, quite sweetly.

"We'll just walk out one side of the tunnel and step into the future. We'll live in whichever horrible world remains."

"You do not mean that," he says.

"I don't mean that," she says.

They eat their dinner as the supports around them groan and strain. They hear grim, ungodly noises reaching downward, as if the land itself aches.

And though they are made for each other, and ready to die for each other, and overjoyed to be in the same place, the war breaking out above becomes too much to pretend to ignore.

Shira says, "For the first time in my life, I am deeply afraid."

"Come here, then," he says. And he pats his lap.

She pats her lap right back. "Being comforted would be nice. But not at the price of power. Why don't you come to me?"

The mapmaker stands, and, instead of moving toward her, he pulls the tablecloth from the table. He does this without skill, a very bad magician. Everything set on it goes flying.

Amid the clatter, he says, "Should we not, then, just meet in the middle?"

"Yes," she says. "In the middle of our middle. In the center of our dinner at the center of the earth."

They sit on the table and put their arms around each other in a deep, satisfying hug.

The candle has gone out in the mapmaker's rough clearing, and the toppled electric lantern has turned itself off.

There is a single lantern left, hung on a bit of steel rebar poking out from the wall. It puts them in the softest of lights, in this very harsh place.

In this way, the pair sit like lovers at the sea's edge, curled together in the sand. They lean farther into each other, feeling the full weight of the war above, both unsure in the moment, from which direction victory comes.

Acknowledgments

A heartfelt and colossal thank-you to Jordan Pavlin, whose commitment to this novel has been without bounds. I cannot thank her enough for her brilliant contributions and editorial advice. Thanks to my agent Nicole Aragi (who read this book when it was still hidden inside another). A truly special thanks to Lauren Holmes for her inexhaustible support and endless good nature, all of it inseparable from these pages. Her help has been an act of true friendship.

My thanks to Joel Weiss, wise counsel and sounding board, now for more than half a life.

For his substantial assistance with research, thank you to Darragh McKeon, a Hunter College Hertog Fellow. To the sailors, Louis Silver and Ari Haberberg, for sharing their know-how with the terrestrially bound. To all the friends and fine folk who came to the rescue with key facts on a wide variety of subjects, especially Dr. Daniel, Wendy Sherman, Isabella Hammad, Kevin Slavin, Mieke Woelky, Silvia Pareschi (who is already busy translating the book into Italian), and Farmer Steve.

At Knopf, I want to thank the amazing Jordan Rodman—

a force from first meeting, as well as Nicholas Thomson, Betty Lew, Claire Ong, Victoria Pearson, Sara Eagle, and the many wonderful people there who have had a hand in this book. And the same goes for Duvall Osteen and Grace Dietshe at Aragi, Inc.

My deepest gratitude to Chris Adrian and Merle Englander for always reading and believing. To John Wray for his generosity and ping pong. To Deborah Landau at NYU for all kinds of unhesitating support.

I'd like to acknowledge the city of Zomba, Malawi, where a critical draft of this novel was written.

And to Rachel and Olivia, who have all my love and give everything its meaning.

FOR THE RELIEF OF UNBEARABLE URGES

Stories

In the collection's hilarious title story, a Hasidic man gets a special dispensation from his rabbi to see a prostitute. "The Wig" takes an aging wigmaker and makes her, for a single moment, beautiful. In "The Tumblers," Englander envisions a group of Polish Jews herded toward a train bound for the death camps and, in a deft, imaginative twist, turns them into acrobats tumbling out of harm's way. *For the Relief of Unbearable Urges* is a work of startling authority and imagination—a book that is as wondrous and joyful as it is wrenchingly sad. It heralds the arrival of a remarkable and inventive storyteller.

Fiction

VINTAGE INTERNATIONAL
Available wherever books are sold.
www.vintagebooks.com

New *from* NATHAN ENGLANDER

kaddish.com

The Pulitzer finalist delivers his best work yet—
a brilliant, streamlined comic novel about a son's
failure to say Kaddish for his father. *Kaddish.com* is a
novel about atonement; about spiritual redemption;
and about the soul-sickening temptations of the
internet, which, like God, is everywhere.

Available February 2019 from Knopf
For more information, AAKnopf.com